KILLERS' HAVEN

When Rad Lobart rode into Lawless, he went in quietly enough. He wasn't just another gambler, or another pioneer, and he wasn't there to stir up trouble. He wanted only one man, dead or alive, a killer who did not even know Rad was still alive. But there were too many vicious killers in Lawless, and it was indeed a strong-minded man who would dare to ride into this helltown, or a man whose desire for revenge transcended any thoughts of fear.

STEPHEN JERVIS

KILLERS' HAVEN

Complete and Unabridged

LINFORD
Leicester

First hardcover edition published in Great Britain
in 2002 by Robert Hale Limited, London

Originally published in paperback as
Bitter Breed by Chuck Adams

First Linford Edition
published 2004
by arrangement with
Robert Hale Limited, London

British Library CIP Data

Jervis, Stephen, *1928* –
   Killer's haven.—Large print ed.—
   Linford western library
   1. Western stories
   2. Large type books
   I. Title II. Adams, Chuck. Bitter breed
   823.9'14 [F]

   ISBN 1–84395–199–1

Published by
F. A. Thorpe (Publishing)
Anstey, Leicestershire

Set by Words & Graphics Ltd.
Anstey, Leicestershire
Printed and bound in Great Britain by
T. J. International Ltd., Padstow, Cornwall

This book is printed on acid-free paper

1

Dangerous Trails

A special dawn breakfast had been served at the hotel in Silver Creek, for the stage to Lawless was due to leave before the rest of the town was awake. It was a long haul across some of the worst country in the territory, and there would be three changes before they made it into Lawless around evening on the second day. Rad Lobart ate his meal seated at the table close to the window, where he could look down into the street and watch the stage when it rolled up to the depot right across the street. There was little light and the buildings on the other side of the street were dim, half-formed blurs.

Ten minutes later the stage rolled up from the depot, slithered to a halt in front of the hotel. The driver, short, white-whiskered, climbed swiftly from the seat, came into the lobby. Rad heard him talking loudly to the clerk, inquiring how many passengers there were that day, for the long run into Lawless.

Finishing his coffee, he checked his watch, reckoned they had enough time left for a smoke and rolled it expertly, sitting back in his chair as he lit the cigarette, drawing the smoke down into his lungs. Acting together with the food he had just eaten, it worked on him as a stimulant. He had arrived in town late the previous evening and had had only five hours' sleep before being called for breakfast, and when he had risen, tiredness had still lain in his bones. Now the energy of the breakfast lifted him and the tiny germ of restlessness began to stir deep into his mind, evoking pictures and sounds in his mind's eye, the long trip across the wide sierras with only the tall buttes lifting from the ochre-red deserts to break the monotony, the smell of smoke in his nostrils when he had made camp on the shores of a small lake that shimmered in the starlight in the shade of the tall pines.

The urge which had forced him on, driving him westward, had overridden most of these things until now, until he had these few minutes in which to let his mind drift back and think over them. The driver came into the dining room, stood just inside the doorway, looking them over, eyes narrowed and critical under the thick, bushy brows.

'All right, gents,' called the other after a moment, 'time we was pullin' out. We've a long ways to go and some of the country out yonder ain't exactly like the kind you know back east.'

Rad got slowly to his feet, crushed out the stub of the cigarette, rubbed the grey ash from the tips of his fingers and moved around the table, heading for the door. His baggage was ready in the lobby. Picking it up, he headed outside for the stage, swung the valise into the rack on top of the coach, then stood on the boardwalk as the rest of the passengers came out. While waiting for breakfast, Rad had learned their names. A stout ranch owner, paunchy and balding, named Allison, and the other two men, Fred Salter, a Pinkerton man, he reckoned, and a banking man named Tollater.

The driver came out close on the heels of the others, glanced up at Rad as the other three men clambered on board.

'Any objections if I ride upstairs with you?' Rad asked.

The other hesitated for the briefest fraction of a second, then shook his head slowly. 'You're welcome, mister, though I reckon I ought to warn you, it gets a mite hot and dusty there once the sun comes up and we hit the trail through Carson Gulch.'

'Guess I'll risk that.' Rad climbed up to the seat beside the driver. Ten seconds later a whip cracked over the backs of the team, the horses lunged forward in the traces and the stage moved off with a rattling of wheels and a creaking of leather, the coach swaying as they drove out of town.

The horses settled down to a steady pace as they left the town behind and the driver sent the long whip snaking out over them only occasionally when the trail led upgrade into the tall rocks. The coach rattled and swayed danger-ously as they swung around the sharp bends in the trail, and here and there they passed through narrow canyons that were so sheer-sided and narrow that Rad had the feeling they would scrape the rough rock if they deviated by so much as a foot to either side. But it was soon evident that the old driver knew every bend and turn in the trail, knew when to let the horses have their heads and when to slow them a little with the hand brake.

'How far to the first change?' Rad asked, conversationally.

'About twelve miles. Couldn't make it any less because of the country. Not so bad now, but the last of the Indians wasn't cleared out until a year ago. Still see a handful wandering the trails around these parts, but they don't take any interest in us now. Guess they know it ain't worth it.'

'You ever had trouble on this run?'

The oldster glanced at Rad out of the corner of his eye, then nodded. 'Some,' he admitted. 'Not much since we stopped haulin' the payroll for the miners in the hills. Reckon they've pulled up stakes and moved on west, where there are better pickin's.' He pulled a thick wad of black tobacco from his shirt pocket, wrenched off a piece with a jerk of his teeth, held the bar out to Rad, then thrust it back again at the other's shake of his head.

Tall cedars closed swiftly about the trail, shortly gave way to thick pine which covered the whole of the lower slopes of the tall hills that crowded in on them from both sides.

'Headin' up into Callon Pass,' said the driver, chewing methodically on the tobacco. 'Pretty long haul. Three miles up and five down.' As he spoke, he leaned forward in his seat, sent the whip cracking down on the backs of the straining horses. The coach jerked forward as they dug their heels in and began the long haul to the crest of the trail. Large rough-hewn boulders littered the trail at this point, and here and there they were forced to slow as thick branches lay across their path, blown from the trees by some recent gale. Loose stones rattled underfoot, flew up against the sides of the stage, kicked high by the flaying hoofs of the horses.

'Seems to me you're in a danged hurry to get to the top,' Rad commented.

'If you got to push the horses, better to do it while the sun's down.' The driver cast a meaningful glance at the sky overhead. There was not a single cloud to be seen and, to the east, the dawn was brightening swiftly now with the sun only just below the horizon, ready to leap out at any moment and flood the world with light and heat.

'See what you mean,' Rad said quietly.

They moved on and up, through a thickening forest. By the time they reached the peak of the trail, they had moved out of the trees and the sun was glinting brilliantly at them, touching the tops of the hills with a bright red glow that contrasted starkly with the deep blue of the sky overhead.

Heading downgrade, the stage rocked turbulently, wheels sliding in the loose shale. Jake, the driver, was forced to use the brake cautiously, but almost continually now, applying it gingerly whenever they headed for a sharp bend in the trail. To one side of them there was now a sheer drop of several hundred feet into the valley that lay below, with a narrow river bright and shiny like a piece of silver wire where it ran among the rocks. Timber on the southern edge of the trail was tall, lodgepole pine, slender trunks that lifted sheer to the heavens, clawing their way up for almost sixty feet. Jake edged the stage expertly around the bends, brake screeching on the wheels, gave the horses their heads whenever they hit a long straightaway that led arrow-straight down the side of the hill.

More hills lifted, but the trail wound through the lower slopes and the high peaks were tall against the blue mirror of the heavens. Now that the sun was well up, the heat began to tell. The day became a punishment to them. Soon, Rad knew what the driver had been talking about when he had maintained that things would be rough on top. They hit a dust bowl shortly after reaching the bottom of the slope, and the horses kicked up a dust cloud that clung to the air and got into Rad's eyes and nostrils, even though he reversed his neckpieces over his nose in an attempt to keep it out.

Jake seemed immune to discomfort. Perhaps, thought Rad, he had grown so used to it over the years that it no longer made any impression on him.

His seamed, weatherbeaten face was thrust forward as he sat hunched in the seat, his body swiftly adjusting itself to every rock and swaying movement of the stage. Short and squat, it seemed that it would need a charge of dynamite to shift him from his seat or loosen the tight-fisted hold on the reins.

When they pulled into the first changing station, situated in the middle of a broad valley, the sun was rising swiftly to the zenith and the heat head was rising equally swiftly to its pent-up intensity. The bridles and metal bits of the reins sent painful flashes into their eyes, and Rad was glad of the chance to step down and stretch his legs while the horses were changed.

'Reckon Jake's in a mighty hurry to get to Lawless,' said the hostler, hitching up the fresh team into the traces. He glanced at Rad out of the corner of his eye, then looked down at the other's belt, noticing the guns in the holsters. 'You goin' through there, too, mister?'

Rad nodded. 'Got a little business to attend to.'

'Guess you know what you're doin',' concluded the other. He tightened a cinch under one of the lead horses. 'Wouldn't advise any man to go there unless he had a mighty good reason for it.'

Rad pursed his lips. 'Heard somethin' about the place back in Silver Creek,' he admitted. 'They say it's a regular hell town.'

'More'n that,' conceded the other. 'It harbours more killers than any other place you can dream up in the whole state. Ain't no law and order there that I ever heard of.'

'There's a man there I'm lookin' for,' said Rad tightly. His eyes were narrowed a little, and from the look on his face the hostler guessed at the nature of the business this hard-faced young man might have in Lawless. 'Leastways, the last I heard, he was around there some place. If he's still there, I reckon I'll be able to find him.'

'Guess from what you say, he ain't no friend of yours,' commented the other, straightening up with a grunt. He rubbed his fingers along the small of his back.

'You guess right. He's a low-down killer.'

'Lawless is full of killers,' advised the hostler. 'Won't be hard to find one there, but whether it'll be the right one is a different matter.' There was a sly look in his eyes as he went on: 'Besides, they stick together like a pack of rats. You try to get one of 'em and you'll get them all on your neck.'

'Thanks for the warning.'

'Figured you might need it,' said the other, moving off a piece and checking the other horses. 'Lawless is no place for a man to ride unless he knows what he's headin' into. And if you're deliberately goin' there lookin' for trouble, it could be worse for you.'

Rad's smile was a thin, wintry thing, a mere twisting of his lips, that did not touch the rest of his face.

Jake came back from the small way post, examined the reins and harness, nodded shrewdly, then clambered back into his seat. Rad climbed up beside him, settled himself in the hard seat.

'Figured you'd had enough of bein' up here,' grunted the other. 'Might be better inside. It'll be tough goin' from here until the next station.'

Rad glanced down at the coach, then shook his head. 'If we hit dust, they'll be forced to keep those windows shut, and it's goin' to be like an oven in there, with no fresh air at all,' he remarked. 'Reckon I'll take my chances up here.'

'Suit yourself.' The whip snapped and they were off at a fast gallop, the fresh horses pulling strongly in the traces, heading out of the way station and on to the dusty trail that wound north-west towards the low range of hills that grew tall out of the flat plain, some ten miles or so on the horizon.

Jake seemed a little more communicative as they proceeded on the second lap of the long journey. It was as if he had been watching Rad closely during the first stage out from Silver Creek, assessing him, figuring out the kind of man he was.

Chewing on the wad of tobacco which seemed to be his constant companion on these long trips, he said, out of the corner of his mouth: 'We won't hit Gunsight, the next station, until shortly before sundown, shack up there for the night. Old Ben Whipple looks after the place. Queer old cuss. Must be all of seventy, but he won't give up the job. Used to be on this run, fifteen years ago, when it was first started, until he got shot up by some hold-up fellas. Couldn't drive the stage then, so they put him in charge of Gunsight. He'll have everythin' ready for us by the time we pull in.'

'You been on this run for some time?' Rad asked, casually.

The other nodded tersely. 'Ever since Ben finished, nearly nine years.'

'Reckon you know Lawless pretty well, then.'

'Guess so. Pull in there every two days or so unless they decide to cancel one of the runs.'

'Ever hear of a man named Pannard, Ed Pannard?'

The other's jaws moved as he chewed on the tobacco, turning the name over in his mind, then he shook his head. 'Not a common name,' he muttered. 'Guess I'd have remembered it if I'd ever heard of it. He a friend of yours?'

'Not exactly. Last I heard of him, he was headed this way, but that was nearly five years ago. Guess he could've ridden on since then.'

'Reckon so.' The other's eyes were narrowed on him for a moment, shrewd and calculating. 'What'd he do? Kill somebody — rustler? Steal your money?'

'None of those things.' Rad rubbed his mouth with the back of his hand. He eased himself a little further into the seat, held on as they careened around a sharply angled bend in the trail.

'Must've been somethin' awful bad for you to trail him for so long,' commented the other. He had turned his head and was staring straight ahead of him now, eyes lidded against the vicious, burning glare of the sun. 'Still that ain't none o' my business. But if you want my advice, mister, once you get to Lawless, tread careful and easy. There's too many men walkin' around there, keepin' an eye on any strangers who come ridin' in. They don't take too well to anybody stepping around like a stray steer with his tail up, lookin' for trouble. Lawless has got the reputation of harbouring every *hombre* who's on the run from the law. Guess that's where it gets its name.'

Rad nodded, pulled his hat forward a little over his forehead, to shield his eyes from the sun glare. It was going to be a long pull into Gunsight, he figured, from what the driver had said, and he leaned back for his own comfort, eyes three-quarter lidded. This way, he could see all there was to be

16

seen and he speculated on the turn of a creek by the side of the trail, or the long, sloping rise of the hills, still some distance away, directly ahead of them, their topmost slopes covered with pine and a sprinkling of maple, the greens blending well with each other, hiding the underbrush in cool shade. He felt drawn inward by the thoughts which seemed to be the heritage of a lonely man, a man who followed that most deadly of trails, which had only vengeance at the end of it. They crossed the rocky bottom of a bone-dry creek and made a wide sweep around the foothills, keeping to the plain, still in the heat of the sun, which was now beginning its slow drop to the western horizon. It burned like a flame on the trail ahead of them, shocking in its piled-up intensity, bringing a bitter, acrid scent to the dry dust that clung to the air, swirling in an ochreous cloud about them. The heat that rolled back from the punished earth was a terrible and persistent thing. Nothing relieved it. There was no shade here. The hills which would have afforded both shade and coolness were still three or four miles away, sliding away to their left.

The other men in the coach had decided to open the windows, to put up with the dust just so long as they were able to get a few breaths of fresh air. As he glanced down, he noticed one man thrust his head out of the window of the swaying coach, sweat glistening on his face. He was blowing hard, obviously finding it difficult to get as much air as he needed down into his lungs.

'Take a good look at the country around here,' said Jake quietly, nodding his head to one side. 'Reckon there are still plenty of outlaws hidin' out here. Those hills yonder are the best part of fifty miles long and half that distance across. Plenty of places where they can shack up and stay clear of the law. Not that there's much chance of getting anybody to go huntin' for men like that. Nobody could hope to cover all that ground, so the law, what little there is in Lawless and Silver Creek, figures that so long as the outlaws don't make too much trouble, it's simpler and easier to leave 'em alone.'

'What do they live on?' Rad inquired.

Jake pursed his lips. 'They nibble a little at the beef on the plains, drive it off and sell it to the hill folk, or even drive it all the way to the railhead. Sometimes there are a few wagon trains headin' through this way and they make easy pickin's for these men. They know by now that the payroll never goes by the stage, otherwise we'd probably be held up more often than we are.'

They swung left as the trail curved away to the south, cut through a narrow pass, out into the open once more, and for the first few miles beyond the hills the trail was fairly smooth and level, so that they were able to make good progress, the horses still pulling strongly.

Five o'clock found them beside a wide, though shallow, stream, where they pulled up to allow the horses time to drink and blow. They stood, head down, jaded by the long haul across rough country. Rad sat where he was, glancing about him, while the other passengers stepped down to stretch their legs, glad of the chance to move around and ease the pincers of cramp which came from sitting so long in the same position. Ahead of them, tall piney slopes pinched in on the trail where it seemed to grow more twisty and narrow, with a sheer wall of rock lifting on one side, extending for the best part of a mile.

Jake grinned. 'It gets worse further up. This is the worst part of the trail we have to cover. Should be easy goin' tomorrow. Clear run all the way down into Lawless.

Fording the river, they trailed up through lodgepole pine which was, in places, so thick that they were unable to see the sky, the matted branches so thick that not a ray of sunlight managed to penetrate them. Here and there they came across treacherous slides which all but blocked the trail and, crossing a wide glen, Rad saw sign of bear and once, a mountain cat perched high in the branches of a tree, spitting down at them as they moved underneath. He had his hand on the butt of his gun, ready to draw and fire if the animal should attempt to leap, but it merely crouched there, eyes gleaming gold and green in the dim light.

The light began fading and the air grew cooler while they were still among the trees, and by the time they came out into the open once more the sun had dipped behind the crests of the mountains that lay perched on the far horizon, leaving only a brilliant burst of red flame to mark the spot where it had gone down. Rad watched as the reds and golds chased each other across the sky, with long bands of colour stretching the whole length of the horizon in front of them, glinting against the darkening purple of the heavens as night came in swiftly from the east and the first bright stars began to glimmer faintly near the zenith.

There was, perhaps, an hour of twilight left to them when they turned a final bend in the trail, headed down a widening track which broadened out as they reached the bottom and, directly in front of them, Rad was able to make out the small cluster of shadowed buildings which was Gunsight.

There was a yellow light spilling into the courtyard from one of the windows as they rolled into the way station and, as they drew to a halt, the door opened and a man stood framed in the light of the doorway. Thankfully, Rad climbed down from the seat, rubbing his back muscles where they had been chafed by the hard wood and the continual swaying motion of the coach. Ben Whipple came out into the courtyard, nodded to Jake.

'Right on time,' he said, consulting a large pocket watch. 'No trouble on the way, I take it.'

'None at all,' affirmed the other.

'Better turn these critters loose and then treat us to some of that fine fare you always seem to provide for us.'

'Sure thing, Jake. How many with the stage tonight?'

'Four. Five includin' me.'

They went into the station while Whipple tended to the horses. When he came back, he motioned them to the chairs set around a couple of tables. 'Won't take more'n ten minutes to have everythin' ready for you, gents,' he called, going through into a back room.

Rad lowered himself gratefully into one of the chairs, looking about him with interest. Evidently Gunsight was the stopping over point for the journey into Lawless, and for the trip in the other direction, too. It was even bigger than he had thought, seeing it from the outside, with a wing built on to the main building, housing the bunks where the passengers and crew slept overnight. It seemed to be a big job for one man, looking after a place like this, yet everything seemed clean, spotless and, when the meal finally arrived, Rad was even more pleasantly surprised. The steak was cooked to a turn, with beans and sweet potatoes and flapjacks to follow, and hot coffee to wash it all down. When the meal was finished. Rad sat back in his seat and rolled himself a smoke, a thing he very rarely did. But the meal had provided him with a little more energy, and he did not feel like turning in at that moment, although Jake had made it clear to all of them that they were due for an early start in the morning.

Getting to his feet, he walked out on to the wide porch, leaned against one of the wooden uprights, smoking slowly, feeling the coolness touch his scorched skin like a balm. This was always the best time of the day, particularly after a long and dusty ride such as that which he had endured during the day.

Overhead the stars were bright in the glittering ferment of the universe, where the Milky Way stretched clear over the inverted vault of the heavens, from one horizon to the other, causing a shimmering glow to touch the nearer objects, picking out details of the station. There was a circular corral on the far edge of the courtyard, and he could make out the shapes of several horses in it; the team which had brought them from the other station, and the fresh set of mounts which would take them on to the next.

There was a faint movement at his back, and he swung round to see Allison, the ranch owner, standing behind him, a cigar thrust between his teeth, the tip glowing redly in the darkness.

'You going to Lawless on business, Mister Lobart?' he asked genially.

'You could call it that, I suppose,' Rad answered.

The other watched him close, his face dark and in shadow. 'I got myself a ranch a couple of miles west of Lawless. Got it pretty cheap, too. Reckon the fella who owned it had had enough of living out here, wanted to get back east as soon as he could. Accordin' to what I've been told, it ain't exactly hospitable country there, but I guess I could've found that out for myself, judgin' by what we came through today.'

'Then why buy a ranch there?' Red asked, curious.

'Found it's the best way of doing business. Always bid well below the market value for a dozen places, then wait for the returns.'

'And where does that leave you?'

'You'd be surprised how often there's one *hombre*, wanting to sell out at a loss, just to get out of the country, or for some other reason that makes it essential for him to raise quick cash. I always make a point of paying cash on the nail. Maybe they want money to pay off an old debt, a gambling loss that's hanging over their heads with the knowledge that they either pay up or they get a bullet in 'em and a shallow grave up on Boot Hill. Maybe they don't like the territory and want to get out while they still have a whole skin. Usually it's none of my business. I just pay rock-bottom prices and step in. If they don't have the guts to work the place, I soon find a way of doing it. Ain't lost a penny yet on any of the deals I've made.'

'You must've made a heap of enemies somewhere along the line.'

The other smiled faintly. 'In this business that's inevitable, a risk you have to take.' Allison gave the idea some thought as he took another cigar from his breast pocket, lit it with the still-glowing butt of the first, sucking in his cheeks as he drew it alight. 'You're not riding into Lawless for the same thing, are you?'

'No.' Rad shook his head, smiling thinly. 'Just looking for a man.'

'Hope you find him,' said the other evenly.

'I will,' said Rad grimly.

'And when you do find him?' asked the other with a quirk of his brows.

'All I want is an even chance with

him and I'll shoot him — and that will be the end of it.'

★ ★ ★

Silence lay around the station; a silence made all the deeper and more intense by the faint night sounds in the distance, the pitiful wail of a loon somewhere up in the hills, lifting his voice to the moon, which had just risen and was throwing a faint yellow pattern of light through the window of the long dormitory. Rad stirred under his blanket, part of his mind awake, listening to the distant sounds.

Five minutes, ten, then full wakefulness came as his ears picked out a distant sound, faint, far away, yet one which intruded on the other sounds; the on-travelling murmur of horses. He lay quite still for a long moment, listening intently. The sound came down to him with the small wind outside, making faint flutters in the air and, acting on impulse, he slipped out of the blankets and moved silently to the window, peering cautiously out into the night. Moonlight laid an eerie white glow over everything. The posts of the corral stood out darkly against the light and he made out the slow moving shapes of the horses on the nearer side, edging restlessly around the fencing. Something had caught their attention, too, he noticed.

He lifted his gaze, peered out to where the tall hills climbed up into the bright, moonlit heavens. The timber showed a dark mass on the crests and he was just able to see the grey-white scar of the trail where it led up in a series of curves over a steep ridge. There was something moving out there, a cloud of dust, he figured, no bigger than a man's hand, but picking out the position of the riders, tightly bunched, as they put their mounts forward at a punishing pace. He drew his lips tightly together. They had passed no one on the trail here, and he doubted if those men out there were abroad for any lawful purpose at that time of the night, riding when no one was out on the trail. He guessed that they were heading down towards the way station, watched their progress, heard the murmur of their horses' hoofs on the hard trail above the faint sighing of the wind around the walls of the building.

A mile away the trail dipped sharply into a hollow, and he lost sight of the riders as they rode down into it. When they emerged once more they had slowed their breakneck pace, were riding in a more leisurely fashion, as if wary now that they were so close to the station. Slipping back to his bunk, he pulled one of the Colts from its holster, checked the chambers, then moved back to the window, crouching down and peering out.

There was a sudden creaking at his back and he heard the springs on one of the other bunks grate in protest as someone woke and eased himself upright. A moment later he heard the soft padding of feet across the floor, and a dark shape crouched down beside him.

'What's goin' on, Lobart?' asked Jake hoarsely, peering over his shoulder into the moonlight.

'Riders — yonder.' Rad pointed. 'Heard their approach a little while ago, must have pulled me out of my sleep. They were hittin' hell for leather a while back, but now they're close to the station they've slowed. Wouldn't surprise me if they didn't haul up and come the rest of the way on foot.'

'Now why in tarnation would they want to do that? Ain't nothin' around here for 'em, if they're lookin' for gold.'

'Not unless one of the other passengers is carryin' somethin' with him,' Rad remarked. 'Come to think of it, Allison did mention that he was on his way to Lawless to buy himself a ranch and some land there. Could be he's carryin' a goodly sum with him. If they got wind of that back in Silver Creek, they may have decided to sneak up on us here and hope to take us by surprise.'

'If that's the case, reckon it's a good thing you heard 'em,' grunted the other. He rubbed his whiskered cheeks with one hand, eyes glittering in the pale moonlight that flooded through the window. 'Reckon we ought to warn the others?'

'Better hold off for a while until we see what those buzzards are up to. No sense in stampedin' them into action if there's no trouble.'

'They've stopped like you said,' muttered the other. He pointed. The bunch of riders had halted on the brow of a rise some five hundred yards from the station. They seemed to be talking among themselves, still in the saddle. Then they swung down, and while one of them led the horses away, the others scattered and began to move forward on foot. Rad reckoned there were perhaps half a dozen of them, easing their way forward from one concealing shadow to another. They came on steadily and stubbornly, evidently working to some prearranged plan, reached the far side of the wide corral and went down out of sight among the moon-thrown shadows there.

Rad tightened his lips, lifted the gun in his right hand to cover the courtyard outside. 'Guess you'd better waken the others, old-timer,' he said softly. 'This looks like trouble, big trouble.'

He waited until the other had crawled away to where the rest of the men were sleeping, then cautiously opened the window, feeling the cold blast of air that swirled through, striking him on the chest and shoulders. He heard the uneasy movements of the horses in the corral as they sensed trouble, kept his gaze moving from one side of the corral to the other, watchful for the first sign of trouble. Those men meant to come at the way station from two sides, he estimated.

'What's happening?' asked Allison sharply, as he came padding across the room. The other two passengers and Ben Whipple were close behind him, the latter carrying an ancient Sharps rifle in his hands. It looked so old that Rad wondered whether it was safe to fire, and even if it were, how accurate it would be.

'There's a bunch of *hombres* sneaking up on the station out yonder,' he said briefly, in a low voice. 'I spotted 'em a few minutes ago. They came down the hill trail yonder.'

'How many of the critters are there?' grunted Ben, hoarsely. He edged forward to take his place at the window, staring out through narrowed eyes into the bright moonlight that flooded the scene in front of them.

'Six, seven maybe. Hard to tell in the light. They're crouched down at the far side of the corral at the moment, maybe working their way around it to take us from two sides. Three of you had better go to the back of the building, keep a sharp look out there. The other two stay here with me.'

'All right, you two,' said Ben authoritatively, getting stiffly to his feet. He motioned to Salter and Tallater with his rifle. 'Let's move. Just hope both of you know how to handle a gun.'

Salter gave a brief nod. A few moments later they had left the dormitory and Rad turned back to the window. A shadow broke from the far side of the corral, ran doubled-over for ten yards or so before dropping down again out of sight. He doubted if the others knew that they were awake and watching, but they were obviously taking no chances. Not until they were in position and ready to attack. He drew his brows together and bit on his lower lip as he tried to figure out in his mind why this attack was being made. Clearly those men would not risk an attack on one of the stage way-stations unless they were reasonably confident they would get something out of it. He could think of nothing that was being carried on the stage on this particular trip which would account for this.

Bending forward, he stared straight ahead of him, unblinkingly. There was nothing to be seen in the near distance. All of the men were still crouched down out of sight, keeping their heads low.

Allison had taken up his position at one of the other windows and abruptly he lifted his gun, aimed it off into the moonlight, and fired a couple of shots. Rad shifted his gaze suddenly, saw the dim shadow which had been on the point of running towards a small clump of trees suddenly pitch forward on to its face and lie still, huddled up in the moonlight.

The echoes of the shots were still atrophying in the distance when the return fire came from the direction of the corral. Above the frightened neighing of the horses, the shots lifted clear into the night, the full volley smashing against the front of the building, splintering wood and smashing the glass in one of the windows nearby. Allison drew his head back sharply, glanced across at Rad, then pressed himself still closer to the wall, flattening himself against it, occasionally risking a quick glance through the window.

Rad aimed and fired swiftly at the muzzle flashes which gave away the positions of the hiding men. He heard one man cry out with a loud and terrible yell as a bullet found its mark, but it was impossible to see just what damage it had done. There was, as yet, no firing from the front of the station. Their own fire had pinned down the men near the corral, making it too great a risk to work their way any further around the building.

There was the rough, tearing impact of lead hitting the wooden ledge of the window just above his head, and he felt the splinters strike him on the head and shoulders as he crouched lower against the wall. Every muscle in him was taut, stretched tight in his limbs, as he listened to the rattle of gunfire pouring into the side of the building. His mind was suddenly very clear and sharp, so that it seemed every tiny sound was magnified out of all proportion, impressing itself on his mind. He followed the shifting of the fight with his ears, knew that some of the men outside were firing at the windows to force them to keep their heads down while the others moved around the sides of the building.

There was a clear, distinct shout outside, hollowly echoing above the gunfire. Carefully, he lifted his head, flinched as a slug hummed through the open window close to his check, droned across the room and embedded itself with a leaden thud in the opposite wall. Looking out, he saw a man edging along the side of the corral fence, head bowed to present a more difficult target, a rifle held in his hands. Even as he spotted the other, the man lifted the rifle sharply to his shoulder and fired, but the bullet struck wide of Rad's position.

Instinctively he snapped a couple of shots at the other, saw the man stagger as one of the slugs hit him. The rifle dropped from his fingers and he threw out an arm, clinging desperately to one of the uprights in an attempt to stay on his feet, as if he knew that once he went down, he would not be able to rise again. Swaying drunkenly, he staggered off into the shadows, stumbling as he lurched forward, one hand up to his shoulder.

Firing now broke out at the other side of the building. Rad was able to hear it as it swung sharply round. But there was no time to worry about the other three men there. They would have to take care of themselves.

There was a sudden interval of quiet. Five minutes passed without as much as a whisper from outside. From the other window, Allison said harshly: 'Maybe they've gone, pulled out when they found we were ready for 'em.'

'Could be but, somehow, I doubt it. We'll be able to tell when they leave. Their mounts are up yonder on the brow of that hill. They left one of their number there with the horses. They have to make their way back there if they want to ride out of here, unless they get their friend to bring the horses down to 'em, and that ain't likely.'

'You're forgettin' somethin',' muttered Jake from the far window. 'If things get really rough for 'em, they can take horses from the corral yonder. Figured they'd do that, anyway, just to stop the stage movin' out tomorrow. Even if we beat 'em off, they won't want news of this to get back to Silver Creek too soon.'

Rad cursed himself for not having thought of that before. True, the corral was in full view of them from here and they would be able to shoot at any man who tried to grab himself a horse from there, but in spite of that, these critters might decide to try for it. Or they might open the gate and hope to drive the horses off by stampeding them with gunfire.

Out of the corner of his eye he glimpsed the head that kept appearing at odd intervals around a pile of wood some two hundred yards away. The distance was a little far for a Colt and, edging back, he took down one of the rifles standing against the wall, checked that it was loaded and crouched down, steadying the weapon on the window ledge. He made a guess as to distance and elevation and drew a thoughtful bead on the spot where he had seen the head. He waited tensely, taking up the trigger's slack. The head appeared once more, lifted cautiously above the woodpile. Rad waited until he had the other's head in the notch of the sights, then let go. The rifle bucked against his wrists and he saw the man fall back, then slip sideways, his body pitching into the dust at the side of the woodpile.

As if his death had been a signal to the other men, a flurry of shots lashed the building. Then they rose up from where they were crouched against the fencing and ran off into the shadows, bending low as they ran, pausing only to send a few scattered shots back at the defenders. Rad sent a single bullet after them, but it missed, and then they were out of range, running along the upgrade trail to where they had left their mounts.

'Guess we scared the critters off,' said Jake, easing himself back from the wall. 'Wonder why they decided to attack the station. Ain't never done a thing like that before. Could understand it if it'd been Indians, but they ain't been on the warpath for years.'

'You haulin' any gold on that stage, Jake?' Rad asked pointedly.

'Dust?' The driver shook his grizzled head. 'Neither gold or money on this trip. You figger that's what they were after?'

'Could've been, I suppose. But why did they wait until we got here, why not hold us up on the trail, where it'd have been easier for them to have taken us by surprise. They made plenty of noise headin' in over the hill trail.'

'Could be they reckoned we'd all be asleep and they could take us before we got hold of our guns,' muttered Allison.

'That must have been it.' Rad stared out through the window, then moved to the door. 'Cover me,' he said shortly. 'I'm goin' out there to take a look at those men we hit. One may still be alive, and if he is, we might be able to make him talk a little. There's somethin' downright funny about this night attack.'

He waited for a moment while Allison and the other moved over to the windows once more, then opened the door and stepped down into the courtyard. The cold breeze sent a little shiver through him, congealing the sweat on his back and forehead. Cautiously, he approached the nearest of the bodies lying face-downward near the corral fence. The man did not move as he reached him and, bending, Rad saw the stain of blood on his shirt as he turned him over. He was already cold. The face was one he did not recognize, lantern-jawed, with the flesh lying close to the bones.

Crossing over to the other two men who lay close together, one beside the woodpile, he found both to be dead. There was no sign of the man he had hit in the shoulder, the man who had staggered off into the darkness. Evidently he had succeeded in reaching his horse up there among the trees.

Going back into the station, he holstered his gun. 'Nothing there that will tell us anything,' he said harshly. 'Typical killers by the look of 'em.'

'Ever see any of 'em before?' asked Jake, eyeing him closely.

'All strangers to me.'

'Plenty of killers in these hills,' went on the other, thinly. 'Maybe they got word from some place that we was carrying a valuable cargo and decided to make a try for it. Only thing I can think of at the moment.'

'You reckon they might be back?' Allison wanted to know.

Rad shrugged. 'Your guess is as good as mine,' he retorted. 'If they figure there's somethin' worth while here, they could bring up more men and attack us again before we pull out at dawn. On the other hand, they might lie in wait for us somewhere along the trail, hoping to hold us up there.'

'That's more probable,' Allison agreed. 'We'd have very little cover out on the trail. Here we could shoot back at them with very little risk to ourselves.'

Whipple came into the room with the other two men at his heels. 'They just faded off into the darkness,' he said in a thin tone. 'I reckon we winged one of 'em before they pulled out.'

Rad glanced round at the other passengers. 'I know this is really none of my business,' he said shortly, 'but are any of you gentlemen carrying anythin' real valuable? Anythin' that these *hombres* could have heard about before we pulled out of Silver Creek?'

One by one the men shook their heads, faces bewildered. Rad guessed that they were telling the truth. He shrugged, eyed Jake from the corner of his eye.

'Then I wonder what those critters were after,' he said harshly. 'It's not usual for them to attack in force like that unless they're pretty sure they'll get somethin' for their pains.'

2

Hold-Up!

For the rest of the night, Rad remained awake and alert, seated at the window which overlooked the courtyard, but there was no further sign of the men who had attacked the station earlier. When the first grey streaks of dawn lit the eastern sky, he got stiffly to his feet, stared down at Jake's whiskered face where he slept in one of the chairs at the other side of the room, then made his way through into the kitchen. Whipple was already there, looking as if nothing had happened, as though he had enjoyed a full night's rest. He grinned at Rad through his beard.

'Thought I'd get up early and fix you all a bite to eat before you move on out,' he explained. 'There's coffee on the stove yonder if you want some.'

Rad poured himself a cup of the steaming coffee, added sugar and condensed milk from the tin, stirred it mechanically, thoughts running over themselves in his mind as he tried to figure things out.

'This sort of thing ever happened before?' he asked, glancing at the other over the rim of the cup.

Whipple shook his hoary head. 'Not since the Indians were on the warpath some years ago. We ain't troubled by the outlaws. They might hold up the stage if they figured it was carrying something worth while, but they do that on the trail. Too risky for 'em to try it here.' His grin widened a little. 'Guess they found that out the hard way last night.'

'Not usual for 'em to take a chance like that,' Rad said, keeping his gaze fixed on the other's face.

Whipple placed a couple of flapjacks on the pile he had already built up, shook his head. 'You're right there, mister. Don't know what got into 'em, pulling a stunt like that.'

Jake came in at that moment, sniffing like a dog getting the scent of a jack rabbit. He gave Rad a friendly nod. 'Guess you didn't sleep much last night, Lobart,' he said, noticing the look on Rad's face. 'If you ask me, they're miles away by now, deep in the hills. They got more than they bargained for when they attacked this place. Reckon they won't bother us no more.'

Rad said nothing. Inwardly, he did not feel quite as sure about that as the other did. While they ate the breakfast which Whipple had provided, the oldster went outside to harness up the fresh team which would haul the stage through the morning to the next stopping place some ten miles further on.

The sun was just lifting above the layer of pine on the hills to the east when the stage finally rumbled out of the dusty courtyard and headed west. Seated up with the driver, Rad held the rifle tightly between his hands, eyes flicking from one side of the trail to the other, alert for trouble.

'You expectin' trouble, son?' asked Jake, turning his head slightly.

'Just bein' prepared,' Rad said. 'We're missing a bet somewhere here. Those *hombres* took a big chance last night, trying to wipe us out like they did. They knew nobody else would happen along the trail at that time of night, but they didn't know how many guns we had with us. That was their mistake, and I figure that if they do decide to try again, they won't make the same mistake twice.'

Jake shrugged. Flicking the whip, he laced it across the backs of the horses, urging them forward at a still greater speed, the wheels of the coach bouncing and jerking as they rolled over the rough track, tilting the stage precariously to one side. Even Jake seemed anxious to be away from Gunsight.

Ten o'clock, with the sun climbing higher into the cloudless blue of the heavens and the heat beginning to tell on them, they were running through tall sandstone bluffs that lifted high on every side. Coarse grass and stunted mesquite bushes were the only living things which grew in this arid desert land, and in places it was almost impossible to make out the trail, where the sand had drifted across it, blown by the searing winds. It was a harsh and inhospitable land. Contemplating it, Rad guessed that it would never be tamed, that nothing could ever be made to grow or flower here. A scar on the landscape which had existed from the dim beginnings of time and would remain the same no matter what men tried to do, no matter how they attempted to change the face of this vast country.

It was high noon before they finally crossed the sandstone wilderness and reached the small way station on the far side, where the low hills lifted up in a series of glens and wrinkles of ground from the plains. Getting down to stretch his legs, Rad was surprised to hear the sound of horses approaching from the opposite direction and a few moments later the eastbound stage rolled into the way station, five passengers getting down. Small as it was, the station had a bar and a place to eat, and they all went inside, out of the heat, while the teams were changed and the coaches made ready.

Rad found himself in conversation with a florid-faced man, sporting a gold watch and chain. The other pursed his lips when Rad asked about Ed Pannard, then shook his head slowly.

'Don't know the name, mister,' he said positively. 'I figure if he was there I'd have heard it at some time or another. I've been in Lawless for close on four years now, know most of the folk there, but that name isn't known to me.'

'Could be he's no longer there,' Rad said thinly. 'Or he may have changed his name. Tall, thin-faced, grey-haired now, I guess, a scar on his left cheek.'

As he gave Pannard's description, he

thought he saw a faint gleam that was more than just interest in the other's eyes, but the man shook his head emphatically. 'Don't know such a man,' he said harshly. 'Guess if he ever did come out to Lawless, he didn't stay around long, or he's got some good reason for staying hidden. Too many men there who're on the run from the law. It's a safe hide-out for killers. Nobody asks questions, nobody comes lookin' for them.'

Rad's smile was thin and wintry. 'This time somebody is comin' looking for one man.' He drained the warm beer in his glass. There was a call from outside, and the passengers for the eastbound stage moved off, filing out through the door and climbing on board. Rad went over to the window and looked out. There was the jingle of trace chains as their team was put into harness.

'Let's get aboard,' yelled Jake briskly. 'Time to be movin' out.'

They boarded quickly and moved off

downgrade at a fast trot, the horses stepping out quickly. Soon they would slow to an even trot but now they were fresh and pulling strongly.

Five miles on the trail levelled and they moved through tall, first-growth pine which shut out the sun, but trapped the heat close to the earth, and held it there, thick and tangible and unmoving. Rad let his body move with the rolling stage. His thoughts were far away as he let his gaze wander into the thick brush beneath the trees. The immediate desire to get to Lawless as soon as was humanly possible had evaporated a little now that they were approaching the end of the trail. Far back in Silver Creek he had felt the urge and the compulsion, the haste to have this thing done with, but with all of the days and hours behind him, he had gradually developed a feeling of cold patience so that time mattered very little now. In spite of what he had heard from those who had been in Lawless, he felt certain in his own mind that Pannard was still there, maybe living under an assumed name, staying in the background, though there was no reason why he should be hiding like that. He doubted if the other knew he was still alive. Even if he did, there was the possibility that he would not even be able to guess at the desire for revenge which lived in his mind.

They forded a narrow, swift-moving creek, the horses splashing through the white-foamed water. In the middle it was deeper than they had imagined from the bank, and the water came swirling around the tops of the wheels, splashing up against the bottoms of the doors. The far bank was steep and stony, and at the very top the trail swung sharply round to enter the timber again. Rocking and swaying precariously, they were forced to slow their pace to climb the bank and move up on to the trail once more, Jake pulling hard on the reins to bring the lead horses around the sharply-angled bend.

As they swung around the bend, Jake hauled tightly on the reins, reaching down for the brake with a sudden yell of alarm as he spotted the fallen tree which lay directly across the trail scarcely ten yards ahead. The sudden jolt threw Rad forward and he was forced to clutch hard at the sides of the seat to avoid being pitched off the stage on to his face. At the same moment a masked rider eased his mount from among the trees, rifle levelled at them.

'Don't make any funny moves with that gun, mister,' he warned sharply, as Rad straightened up, swinging up the barrel of the Winchester. 'This is my drop.'

Slowly, Rad let the Winchester fall to his side, stared hard at the other, watching the unwinking eyes that stared up into his from above the mask.

Carefully, the rider edged his way forward, said in a sharp tone as the door of the stage was forced open: 'Don't any of you men in there make a funny move. There are more rifles lined up on you from the trees.'

Without moving his head, Rad swivelled his gaze, saw that the other spoke the truth. He could just make out the shapes of the other men among the trees, covering them from both sides. It was a cleverly executed trap and they had ridden right into it. They had no choice but to do just as the other said.

Tight-lipped, he watched as the leader came forward, keeping the rifle levelled on his chest.

'Just what is this?' demanded Jake throatily. He glared at the men. 'We ain't haulin' no gold or money this trip. If you'd taken the trouble to ask around in Silver Creek you'd have known that.'

'We know,' snapped the masked man with the brushy chin. As he spoke, the three men stepped down from the coach with their hands lifted high. 'We ain't lookin' for gold.' His eyes searched the faces of the men who stood by the coach, and then lifted back to Rad.

'Your name Lobart?' he asked tightly.

'That's right.' Rad felt a little

unpleasant thrill of surprise run through him.

'Figured it might be.' The other nodded as if in secret understanding. 'All right, you'd better step down and come peaceful like, unless you want these men to get shot.'

Rad clambered down, stood with his back against the stage, staring up at the masked man. He was still completely in the dark as to what was happening and what these men could want with him. But it seemed they knew who he was, even though that made little sense as yet.

'Move off along the trail,' snapped the leader harshly. 'Unbuckle that gunbelt first.'

Rad was forced to obey. One look at the man's face told him that it had been no idle threat when he had said he would kill the others if he did not do as he was ordered. He let the gunbelt fall to the ground, then walked off slowly along the trail to where the tree lay across it.

'Haul it to one side,' ordered the outlaw roughly.

Bending, Rad grasped the sapling and pulled with all of his might, dragging it off the trail and back into the brush. Straightening up, he watched while the outlaws forced the rest of the men to discard their weapons and toss them into the brush. Then they unharnessed the horses and sent them stampeding along the trail.

'Guess you'll have to walk the rest of the way to the next post,' said the leader with a mocking grin. He gigged his mount back to where Rad was standing by the trail. 'As for you, Lobart, you come with us. Now start moving along that side trail yonder.' He pointed with the rifle.

Rad turned. A dim, rutted trail led up through the trees into a narrow tributary ravine of the creek. Slowly he made his way forward, aware that the other men were following, watching his every move. To Rad, this did not make sense. He reckoned these were part of the same party that had attacked the way station.

Pausing as he came to the edge of the creek, narrower at this point than where the stage had forded it, Rad turned to face the men behind him. 'If you figure I've got anythin' on me worth stealin', you're making a big mistake,' he gritted.

The leader leaned down from the saddle and prodded him roughly with the barrel of the Winchester. 'Just keep walkin',' he ordered.

Rad sucked in his breath as the blow took all of the wind from his lungs, tightened his lips and stumbled forward, splashing his way through the swift-flowing water, feeling the current drag at his legs as he made his way across. Reaching the other side, he clambered up the stony bank on to the narrow trail, moving through the trees. It was soon clear that this trail had not been used for a considerable time. Overhanging branches slashed at his head and face as he pushed his way through them, ducking low to avoid others that threatened to decapitate him. Behind him, he heard nothing. There was nothing that Jake or any of the others could do to help him. This was clearly none of their business and although they would report the matter to the Sheriff in Lawless once they got there, Rad doubted if that would do him any good. These men had not taken him off that stage for the good of his health.

About a mile from the stage route the rutted trail led out through the trees, widened as it entered a broad ravine. Around a corner there was a clearing, and in the centre a crude log cabin with a provision cellar close by, sunk in the ground. The samples of rock and ore scattered around suggested that it had once been owned by a prospector. Now it seemed to have been deserted for some time, but as he reached it, and the men climbed down from their horses, he noticed that the small corral fence had been newly repaired, and inside the cabin there were sacks of food on the table and several bunks in one corner.

'Get inside,' ordered the leader, swinging down from the saddle. He kept the rifle trained on Rad. Lowering his head, Rad stepped through the narrow, low doorway. It was dark inside the shack, and several minutes passed before his eyes grew accustomed to the dimness.

'All right,' Rad said, forcing evenness into his tone. 'You've got me here. Now maybe you'll explain what this is all about. Like I said, I ain't carrying gold or valuables.'

'Reckon there's no harm in tellin' you now,' assented the leader. He pulled the mask from his face, grinned viciously at Rad, eyes narrowed. 'We got the tip-off that you were in Silver Creek, maybe headin' this way. There's somebody in Lawless wants to see you, but he didn't want to meet you off the stage. Seems he reckons you could be dangerous to him. So he asked us to grab you before the stage got into town.

Guess he reckoned you might go gunning for him, and he likes the odds stacked in his favour. He never banks on anythin' but a sure thing.'

There was a minute of hollow silence, then Rad nodded his head slowly. It was beginning to figure in his mind. 'So that's how it is,' he said softly. 'I was beginning to wonder. That raid on the way station at Gunsight last night was an attempt to take me then?'

The other's face hardened. 'We lost three good men,' he said through his teeth. 'If it wasn't that we were told to take you in alive, I'd shoot you down here and now, then go back for those others on the stage.'

'You expectin' me to walk all the way into Lawless?'

'We'll get you there,' the other promised confidently. 'When the others get here, they'll have a mount for you.'

'What do we do with him in the meantime?' grunted one of the others. 'Smiley won't be here for another hour or so.'

'He won't give us any trouble,' muttered the leader. He went over to a door at the end of the cabin, unlocked a padlock, took down the wooden bar which had been placed across it and swung the heavy door open. Rad saw that it led into the sunken dugout.

'Inside here,' ordered the other harshly.

Moving forward, Rad saw that the earthen steps led down into the small dugout, steep beyond the door. Ducking his head, he hesitated in the opening, trying to see into the pitch blackness that lay beyond. The butt of a rifle hit him hard and viciously across the back of his knees, pitching him into the hole. He fell heavily, his legs twisting under him, arms thrown out in an attempt to break his fall. There was a mocking laugh as the door slammed shut behind him. He heard the sound of the wooden bar being slid into place, followed by the padlock. Groping his way to his feet, he sucked in a harsh breath as his skull cracked painfully against the low ceiling of the dugout.

In the darkness, he managed to reach the door, threw himself against it, but it had been deliberately made thiefproof and the stout oaken slats resisted all of his efforts. It was impossible for him to stand up straight and finally he gave up the attempt to break down the door, and sank down on to the cold, earthen floor, rubbing his legs where they had been twisted under him as the outlaw had thrust him down into the dugout.

There was the smell of stale and decayed food in the air, stinging the back of his nostrils, and for the first time he began to contemplate the full seriousness of his situation, wondering how long these men intended to keep him locked down there. The dugout was about as airtight as it was possible to make it, and the staleness bore testimony to the fact that very little fresh air managed to get in. He would suffocate if they didn't come for him soon.

It was, perhaps, more than an hour

before he heard the rattle of the key in the padlock and the door was pulled open. He blinked in the sudden glare of red sunlight which slanted through one of the windows of the shack and fell full in his eyes. For a moment there was a sharp throbbing pain at the back of his eyes, then it went away slowly and he stood up, sucking air down into his lungs, aware of the sweat that had formed on his forehead and neck. There was a stranger with the bunch, Rad noticed. Evidently this was Smiley, the man they had been waiting for, bringing the extra horse.

Rad thought fast. Once these men got him into Lawless, there was no chance for him. His only hope lay in being able to escape on the way into town, and he knew he couldn't do that in broad daylight, even with the light fading slowly. He had to play for time. In the darkness there might be a chance.

'You figurin' on makin' me ride out without any grub?' he demanded.

The other stared at him for a long moment with no expression on his face. Then he grinned viciously. 'I guess we can afford to let you have somethin' to eat before we pull out,' he said. He winked broadly at the rest of the men standing in the background. 'After all, there'll be plenty in store for you once we get you to Pannard. It'll be somethin' you can look forward to while you're eating. Rustle him up a bite of grub.'

One of the men moved away to the rear of the shack, brought out some dried beef and a mug of lukewarm coffee which seemed to have been boiling over the fire in the stove far too long so that all of the taste had gone from it, and there was only a burnt taste to it. Rad seated himself at the small table, aware of the men watching him closely. He chewed slowly on the dried meat, washing it down with the coffee. It was unappetizing fare, but he knew he would get nothing better from these men, and if he could delay them for half an hour or so, he might be able to give them the slip on the trail into Lawless. Outside, the sun went down behind the hills with a vivid red flash, like some distant explosion over the edge of the world, and the purple and black came rushing in swiftly from the east to swamp out the golds and blues.

Smiley said tautly: 'Reckon we'd better ride, Clem. Gettin' dark now and that ain't the best of trails, even in daylight. There's a break about two miles from here, maybe a hundred feet from the bottom. We don't want to get caught on that in the dark.'

'We'll make it all right,' said Clem impatiently. He turned to Rad: 'All right, you've had your bite to eat. Now on your feet and move outside.'

The horses were tethered to the small rail in front of the shack and Rad was pushed towards one of them, the barrel of a gun hard in the small of his back. He climbed stiffly into the saddle as Clem mounted up. Then the other eased his horse across to Rad's.

'Cover this *hombre*, Smiley,' Clem ordered, 'while I tie his hands behind his back. I ain't taking any chances with him.'

'You reckon that's wise?' muttered Smiley, levelling his gun on Rad's chest. 'A man can't handle a horse across that break with his hands behind him.'

'He'll handle this one, or go over the side,' said Clem grimly.

He lifted the length of rope which he had taken from his saddle, motioned to Rad to hold his hands behind his back, and lashed his wrists together, pulling the rope more tightly than was really necessary. Rad felt it bite into the flesh of his wrists, tried to hold them as far apart as possible, so that once he drew them together, it would slacken the rope a little and give him a better chance of wriggling out of them. In addition, they had not taken the precaution of searching him properly, evidently believing that so long as he was not wearing a gunbelt, he was unarmed. Consequently, they had not discovered the sharp-bladed hunting knife in his rear pocket.

'Guess that ought to hold until we get you into Lawless,' said Clem, nodding. He wheeled his mount, threw a quick glance at the darkening sky, then motioned to the rest of the men to form up into single file. Ahead of them the trail was a narrow grey scar on the rocky ground that led away from the shack, running level for perhaps a couple of hundred yards, before dipping sharply downward and twisting out of sight around the edge of a large upthrusting boulder.

The light died out while they were still on the level section of the trail, and from that point on they were forced to allow the horses to pick their own pace down the side of the mountain or it would have been a short cut to hell for all of them. There was no room to ride two abreast on this trail. The canyon had steep sides which hemmed them in on both sides, and Rad felt a momentary disquiet at the idea of riding over a break in the trail, unable to hold on to the reins or guide his mount except by using his knees and legs. He swayed forward in the saddle to make it easier on himself and the horse when they reached the break, letting his gaze drift ahead and to both sides of him, mind working as he tried to figure out when to make his attempt at breaking away from these men. He wasn't sure how far it was into Lawless by this route, and he felt a restless impatience bubbling up inside him.

There were two men riding at his back, Smiley and one of the others, with Clem leading the way, almost out of sight at intervals as the trail swung around sharp turns, and intervening boulders got in the way. With an effort, he managed to lift his arms slightly so that his fingers touched the pocket behind him. There was little feeling left in his hands because of the tightness of the rope around his wrists, and although he worked hard with his fingers, it was several minutes before he managed to slide the knife from his pocket and flick the blade into position.

The horse he rode was, fortunately, a sure-footed brute, made wary it seemed by long acquaintance with this particular trail. When it came up against the break, it halted. Clem and the men in front of him had moved out on to the broken ground where the trail had crumbled and slid away from the smooth rock face. They paused on the far side and, in the dimness, Rad saw Clem turned in the saddle, peering back at him.

'Come on over,' he yelled harshly. 'We haven't got all night to wait for you to move.'

Using his knees, Rad edged the horse forward, still keeping a tight grip on the knife behind him. The horse took a tentative step, stopped again as its foreleg hit the loose shale that slid treacherously under it. It drew back and emitted a harsh blast of air through its nostrils, stood trembling for a moment, then went forward once more as he dug spurs into its flanks, striving to guide it with his knees. The trail here was a narrow shelf, less than four feet wide at its greatest width. For a moment the horse slithered sideways as its feet went from under it and, acting on instinct, Rad threw himself to one side, easing in the saddle.

Suddenly the horse found firmer footing at the far end of the break, took a wild lunge forward, heaving itself on to the trail, almost unseating him in the process. He swayed in the saddle, half fell and only succeeded in righting himself with a tremendous effort, almost losing his hold on the knife as he did so.

A quick glance over his shoulder showed the other two men edging their mounts gingerly along the break, and he knew he would not have a better chance to try to free his hands than this, when they were too concerned with their own safety to bother with what he was doing. Tilting the knife, he managed to thrust it hard into the rear of the saddle, where the handle caught, held fast. Desperately he thrust his bound wrists against the blade, rubbed them along it, striving to keep his flesh away from the honed edge of the blade. Even though the horse was standing absolutely still, such was his haste that he felt the cold touch of steel on his wrists and there was the sticky warmth of blood flowing down his hands as he struggled to cut through the rope. The knife was as sharp as constant honing could make it, and the strands of the tough rope were no match for it, as they fell away one after the other. The nearer of the two men was almost at the end of the break, less than three yards from him, when the rope finally parted and his hands were free. He remained absolutely still in the saddle, resisting the urge to rub his chafed and bleeding wrists, knowing that the men at his back would be watching him closely now.

Clem's voice drifted down from the

darkness of the trail. 'You over yet, Smiley?'

'Just got across, Clem,' the other called back. 'Is Lobart all right?'

A pause, then Smiley said harshly: 'He's all in one piece, Clem. Reckon he's thinking ahead to what's in store for him in Lawless.' He laughed tonelessly.

They moved forward along the trail, which was widening appreciably now, as they neared the bottom. Ahead of them the ground seemed more open and Rad guessed they would soon hit the main stage trail into Lawless. The trail played out through gravel and tumbled rocks to the plain below. There was a creek running alongside it now, and the surface of the water held a thin glow in the darkness. The starlight laid a faintly shimmering light over everything, the trees that grew tall along the trail standing out like ghostly sentinels with their trunks and branches held up stiffly to the sky like hands.

A little distance along the trail, Clem

hauled up, rode back to Rad, drawing alongside him. He motioned Smiley up. 'Ground's pretty open up ahead,' he said shortly. 'Better tie a rope on to his bridle. Give him a bit of slack and we can all ride ahead of him.'

'You don't figure he's likely to get away, do you?' said Smiley harshly, his teeth showing faintly in his shadowed face.

'I'm takin' no chances with him,' declared the other stubbornly. 'Now lash that riata to the pommel of his saddle and make it good and tight. I don't want it workin' loose before we hit town.'

Grumbling under his breath, Smiley pulled his riata from the side of his saddle, uncoiled it and fastened one end securely to Rad's pommel, taking the other end and fastening it to his own saddle. 'I guess that ought to hold,' he said tautly. He rode up with the others, the rope tightening behind him, linking Rad's mount with his own.

In the darkness, it was just possible

for Rad to make out the dim shapes of the others as they rode ahead of him, forcing their mounts to a brisk pace. Rad was forced to keep up with them but now he was able to move his hands around from behind him, massage them a little to get the blood flowing through his veins once more. Clem had deliberately tied them so that the blood flow was all but cut off completely.

Ten minutes later the moon came up, lifting from the eastern horizon, sailing up into the starlit heavens. Tightening his lips, Rad turned his head from one side to the other, looking for a chance to escape from his captors. The ground was open, but rough off the trail, and he knew that, whatever happened, he could not stay with the trail for long once he made a break for freedom. He would have to wait for a spot where he could ride off the trail into the shadows, but with the ground open and smooth enough for him to give his mount its head. He guessed he would have perhaps two hundred yards of a start on these men before they realized what was happening and came after him.

After a short, quick rise, the trail entered timber, thick and dense on either side, and Rad forced himself to relax in the saddle. There was no chance here. A rider would be bogged down within seconds of entering that tangled underbrush. The fact made him remain quiet in the saddle until they came out of the timber. A small wind blowing off the crests of the mountains flowed against him as they rode out of the trees, and a quick, all-encompassing glance showed him that here the ground stretched away to his left in a series of smoothly undulating curves which rose and fell all the way to the seeable horizon. To the right the ground remained more rocky, climbing a little towards the bottommost ridges of the mountains. Bending forward in the saddle, he slashed through the rope with the hunting knife. It parted, fell to the ground and began trailing. As yet Smiley had noticed nothing amiss, and abruptly Rad pulled his horse's head around and rode it swiftly off the trail, kicking viciously at its flanks with his spurs, sorry for the animal as he did so, but knowing that he had no other choice. He kept his head low, lying over the saddle. For several seconds, as he rode, pounding into the darkness, there was no sound from behind him. Then, as they hit the rougher ground to the side of the trail, he heard a hoarse yell of warning lifted at his back.

'He's gettin' away, Clem,' said Smiley's voice, high-pitched.

A shot sounded five seconds later but it went wild. They had evidently lost him for the moment now that he was off the trail. He heard Clem's voice yelling orders, caught the thunder of hoofs as they put their horses off the trail, spreading out in a wide arc to hunt him down. He gave his mount its head. Smiley had made a mistake when he had given Rad this particular horse. It was a thoroughbred and, as such, Rad reckoned it would outrun any of the other horses which the outlaws were riding. But they were armed with guns and he was not, and that tended to level the odds a little.

Ahead of him there was a narrow ravine that dipped down into the ground, as if the rock had been scooped out here by some gigantic shovel. He deliberately put his mount down into it, rode along it for a little way, the rocky walls rising on either side until they were above the level of his head. Reining up, his mount slithered to an abrupt halt, breathing heavily in great snorts. Behind him there was no sound. For a moment he wondered what could have happened to the others. Then the realization came to him that they, too, had deliberately halted their mounts and were striving to pick up the sound of his headlong flight, having lost sight of him in the darkness. Leaning forward in the saddle, he placed his hand over his horse's nostrils, whispering gently to it, to prevent it from making any sound if it became aware of the presence of other horses in the vicinity.

Then, out of the darkness, perhaps thirty yards away, off to one side of the narrow ravine, a voice said sharply: 'He must be hiding up somewhere close by, Clem. He can't have run far in this darkness.'

'Then start lookin' for him.' Clem's voice came from some distance away, and although he tried to peer into the moon-thrown shadows, Rad could make out nothing of the others, even though he knew where they were.

There was a delay of almost a minute, during which his pursuers remained still and quiet, clearly searching with eyes and ears for any sign of him. Then a single shadow from a patch of darkness came slowly over open ground, shown up by the flooding moonlight. Rad saw a match flare and make a brief spluttering of red light, saw the man's face vaguely as a grey blur, but did not recognize which of the men it was. The man edged his mount forward slowly, heading in Rad's direction. He stopped when he was less than twenty yards away from the end of the ravine, seemed to be lifting himself up in the saddle as he tried to see, trying to penetrate the darkness with his glance.

Rad feared that his own mount would make some move as the silence grew long. The man seemed to be staring straight at him, and it seemed incredible that he could not see him.

At last the other grew weary of his stance, jerked on the reins and hauled his horse back, away from the open ground, as if he was aware that he could be seen clearly from any of the shadows that massed around him. He must have realized, too, for the first time that Rad had a knife, otherwise he would not have been able to free himself from that riata.

'No sign of him this way.'

'Spread out and move forward. He's got to be here some place.' Clem's tone sounded worried now. Rad could guess what would happen if they were forced to ride back into town and admit to Pannard that they had caught him and then allowed him to slip through their fingers. The man edged back into sight. Casting about him, Rad was just able to make out the shape of another rider, fifty yards or so away, walking his horse slowly forward.

Soon, their strategy was clear to Rad. They would move a hundred yards or so further on and then swing round, circling back, knowing he could not be more than a couple of hundred yards ahead of them, stopped somewhere just out of sight, maybe watching their moves from the darkness of some concealing shadow. One glance was enough to tell him that he would be trapped once they began their back-swing, and it was inevitable they would locate the ravine in which he was hidden.

Very slowly and carefully, he edged his mount to the far end of the ravine, where it was just possible for him to peer into the dimness on either side of the rocky walls. He tried to catch an upward glimpse of the terrain behind him, but his field of vision was too limited and he could make out nothing beyond the serrated edges of the rock. For a moment he remained there, fast-thinking. In a few more moments he would be discovered and a sudden yell would bring all of the men down on him, cutting off any way of escape he might have. Clem and the others had now swung across, were to the north of him, moving slowly in a wide, well-spaced line, searching diligently, peering into every possible cover for any sign of him. Presently they would begin their swing, and this ravine which had earlier afforded him much-needed cover would become a trap.

Catching the reins in his left hand, he bent forward over the horse's neck, threw a quick sideways glance at the men in the distance, then slapped the horse out of the ravine, crouching low in the saddle. He was thirty feet from the ravine, running swiftly over open ground in the moonlight, before he heard the quick, harsh yell from behind him. A bullet struck to the side of him, riccocheting off a rock, whining thinly into the distance with the screech of tortured metal. By the time the firing swung over to follow him, he was riding headlong over coarse grass.

As if it realized the urgency, the horse plunged forward at a breakneck pace. Here and there it almost stumbled in gopher holes and shallow depressions in the softer ground which could not be seen before they were directly on top of them.

Once the horse went down on to its knees as it slithered in a hole and Rad braced himself in the saddle, sliding his feet from the stirrups to prevent himself from being thrown over its head, ready to step down in an instant. But somehow the animal righted itself, struggled upright, continued forward, rising supremely to the occasion.

In any race such as this, Rad would have backed a thoroughbred to outpace any of the horses which were ridden by his pursuers. So it proved as they headed northwest, with the moonlight flooding intermittently about them. A quarter of a mile further on he ran into thick timber, with a dim, narrow trail winding through it. Branches, slender and snake-like, whipped across his head and shoulders, but he ignored them. Some gunfire continued to follow him, but the men were firing blindly, could not hope to see him in the tangled thicket. The timber made a long, slow curve into darker country. He veered into more undergrowth, followed the path until it came out of the trees, ran along the edge of a meadow and saw, in the distance, the yellow gleam of light that showed through the windows of a ranch house. Turning with the meadow's gradual bend, he found himself close to the ranch and, glancing back over his shoulder, he found himself sheltered from the men at his back. He guessed them to be still somewhere in the thick tangle of brush and roots, working their way through the stretch of timber. He reined up his mount and studied his situation and looked about him. The meadows made a long, gentle curve into the hills that stood out in the distance. Beyond them, he reckoned, lay Lawless.

If he tried to run for town, it was possible that the men at his back would be able to cut him off. After all, they knew this country, knew every trail there was, and it was just possible they would know of one which was shorter than that he was forced to follow. On the other hand, would anyone at this ranch care to step up against those men, for he did not doubt that they would head for the ranch before going on, knowing that he might have put up there.

He headed for the ranch house. The trail at this point grew level, moved over gravelly stones, passed through a short stretch of grass. He topped the low rise which lay in front of the house. The length of the barn to one side lay in front of him, all dark, but there was a handful of horses in the corral that faced the courtyard. He skirted this, turned into the courtyard itself, reined up in front of the porch, cocked his ear for any sound in the distance at his back, but heard nothing but the quiet rush of the breeze.

Then the door opened and someone stepped down into the porch. He noticed at once that there was no light in the doorway. Evidently they were wary folk around these parts, and probably with good cause. The shadow stepped forward and he caught the faint gleam of the moonlight on the barrel of a Winchester, pointed directly at him.

'Who's there?' asked a woman's voice.

'Sorry to trouble you, Ma'am,' he said quietly. He saw her move forward a little and give him a stone-still glance, the barrel of the rifle never wavering from him. 'But there's a handful of men on my tail and they — '

For a moment, she peered up at him,

trying to see the expression on his face, then she seemed to be satisfied by what she saw, for she said quickly: 'Into the house. Let your horse into the corral.'

He slid quickly from the saddle, knowing there was little time to lose. Slapping the horse on the flanks, he urged it into the small corral, closed the gate on it, then ran towards the house. As he ran, he heard the girl call orders to the three men who had stepped into the yard from the bunkhouse. In the dark doorway he turned, threw a quick glance over his shoulder. The girl was moving towards him and the three men had slipped away into the darkness of the bunkhouse.

The girl closed the door, but did not lock it. He eyed her curiously and she said in a low, rich voice: 'They will know you have come here, but they won't dare to force their way in.'

'Are you big enough to stop them?' he asked incredulously. 'There are five or six of them and they want me real bad.'

She showed him a lift of her chin and said tightly: 'I can handle this. Just stay out of sight.'

Rad moved into the room at the end of the passage. The girl went out again towards the door and, killing the lamp on the table, he moved across to the window, still unsure of her ability to handle these killers. He heard the sound of riders approaching fast, then Clem's voice lifted high as the bunch of men rode into the courtyard, drawing rein in front of the porch.

Rad heard the front door open, then pressed himself flat against the wall near the window, peering out. He saw the girl step out on to the porch, still gripping the Winchester in her hands. She faced the men fearlessly.

'What do you want here, Blander?' she called. 'We don't encourage your kind at the Bar X.'

'We're looking for a fugitive, Miss Ella,' answered the other. 'Caught him running off some of our cattle up in the hill pastures. Those men with him got clean away, but we managed to follow his trail and it led right here.'

'You claiming you're following a rustler?' There was naked disbelief in the girl's voice. 'I don't believe you, Blander. I know your kind.'

'Now we don't want to have to make any trouble for you,' said the other, with some of the steel beginning to show through his voice. 'But we mean to get this hombre and if you decide to try to stand in our way we'll just have to come inside and take a look-see for ourselves. I'm sure Pannard won't like to hear of you tryin' to stop us.'

'You know my feelings about Ed Pannard,' snapped the girl. She lifted the rifle threateningly. 'Now ride on out of here.'

'So he is hidin' there in the house,' said Clem harshly. 'We might have figured he was the kind to take refuge behind a woman's skirts.' He made to say something more, then stopped abruptly, swayed sideways in the saddle as the girl pressed the trigger of the rifle, sent a slug burning its way along his cheek. For a moment he sat there, with one hand lifted to his face. Then he lowered his arm and stared down at the faint smear of blood on the back of his hand before making to get down from the saddle.

'Now that wasn't a nice thing to do,' he said ominously. 'You've tried to stand against us a mite too long and I figure it's time that — '

'Before you do anything foolish, I'd advise you to take a look around you. There are more than a dozen guns lined up on you this minute. I've only got to give the word and you'll all be shot.'

Clem spun in the saddle, peered about him, pushing his sight into the darkness and the shadows that lay around the barn and the bunkhouse. Then he stiffened in the saddle, said through his teeth: 'All right, you win this round. But it ain't the end of this. We know that you're shelterin' him there and the next time we come you'd better not try to stand against us.'

Wheeling his mount with a savage pull on the reins, he rode out of the courtyard, his men trailing behind him. Rad watched them go, listened to the abrasion of their hoofbeats fade into the night. Then the door behind him opened and the girl came into the room, walked over to the table and lit the lamp once more, the yellow light filtering into every corner of the room.

'You'll be safe here,' she said quietly. There was a firm assurance in her voice which surprised him a little. He wondered where her father was; certainly she didn't run this place by herself, he reflected. Yet Clem had made no mention of a man here, had actually threatened *her* when they rode back.

'Maybe your father wouldn't want me to stay,' he said softly. 'Those *hombres* will carry out their threat and head back soon, bringing more men with them.'

She faced him over the room's length and he thought he saw something at the back of her eyes which he had not noticed before. A hard look, as if there was some memory in her mind which she would have preferred to forget. Then she said in a curiously strained voice: 'My father is dead. He was found shot in the hills a couple of months ago. I run the ranch now and those men know it. There have been some of our cattle missing since my father's death, but so far I haven't been able to pin it on to them.'

Rad nodded. 'You mentioned a man called Pannard, Ed Pannard. Do you know him?'

He saw by the tightening expression on the girl's face that she did. 'He's the one behind all of this,' she said tightly. 'These hills are full of men who kill for the sheer joy of it. Most of them take their orders from Pannard.'

Rad said in a gritty voice: 'I've been lookin' for this man myself for several months now. I heard he was somewhere around Lawless, but when I asked in Silver Creek, nobody knew of him, even men who lived in Lawless claimed they had never heard of a man by that name.'

'I can understand that,' said the girl. 'Men are careful of people like Pannard. He's a ruthless killer.'

Rad felt a tightness in him at the girl's words, but he said nothing more. He knew she was watching him, waiting for him to make some move. Then she said: 'Do you know my name?'

He shook his head. 'I heard one of those men called you Miss Ella,' he said simply.

She came across the room until she stood close to him, said in a low voice: 'Ella Redden. My father started this ranch thirty years ago after coming here from back east. I was born here. He wanted me to go back east for schooling, but this has been the only home I've ever known. Now I'm glad I stayed. I know how to run it and the men who came with my father have stayed loyal to me. That's why I knew Blander would do nothing, even though he probably knew you were here.' She looked out through the window, curiously indrawn and sober. When she spoke again her voice had a drag of sadness to it.

'I don't know why you came here, or why those men were riding you down like that. I do know that you're no rustler as they tried to say you were. Men do things for a great many reasons, but the fact that you asked about Ed Pannard around Silver Creek means to me that you're either a man I ought to shoot down here and now, or you've got a score to settle with him and, if so, then I should do everything I can to help you, even if it may mean that you'll ride into far bigger trouble than you can handle.'

'Better be careful of joining in on this quarrel,' he warned.

She smiled as if in secret amusement. 'This has been my quarrel ever since my father was killed,' she said tightly. 'But what are you going to do now?'

'Ride on into Lawless.'

She remained silent over a long period at that remark, then said in a soft voice: 'Ride into Lawless and I may not even be able to help you. Here, I can call on a great many men to help me. If I say so, they would kill any man riding on to this spread. But Lawless is full of the wild ones. Pannard is only one killer there among a host of others.' Her voice stiffened. 'You must want to kill Ed Pannard very much.'

He nodded jerkily. 'He did something in the past that I cannot forget, that I cannot forgive. For that, I swore he would die.'

'I can understand that,' said Ella Redden, after considering him for a while. 'I felt like that when they brought my father back after finding him in the hills. I know Pannard had a hand in it. He swore he would pay my father back for not selling out to him when he offered to buy the ranch.'

'But you had no proof that he did it?'

'No, he was too clever for that. Not

that it would have made much difference. There is no law in Lawless except the law of the sixgun. Ride into town and you'll soon find that out for yourself, if you live that long.'

'This is something I have to do,' he told her fiercely. He was smiling a little, but there was a tightness to his face which she did not fail to notice.

'Then stay here for a little while,' she pleaded. 'Go riding blindly into Lawless and you'll never get away from trouble.'

3

Troubled Range

A man came riding down from the hills some time before noon the next day, riding on an old grey horse, which stood with its head bowed in the middle of the courtyard as the man went inside the house. He gave Rad a sharp-bright stare as he noticed the other, seated on the crossbar of the corral fence.

'Looks like trouble in Lawless,' observed Cal, one of the Bar X hands. 'That's Al Sullivan.'

'That where he comes from?'

'That's right. He acts as Miss Ella's eyes in town. Reckon he never misses anythin' that happens there.'

Rad remained seated on the topmost rail of the corral, from where he could watch the house and everything around it. There was a tight silence over the place, he decided, born of apprehensive fear and mistrust of the people in town.

He thought back over what had happened to him since leaving Silver Creek, wondered whether Ed Pannard knew who he really was and the reason why he was heading into Lawless. There had been that time some nine months back when he had raised a smell of the other about a hundred miles to the east, when he had been working in one of the railroad camps laying the gleaming rails west where they would eventually link up with California. Maybe Pannard had put two and two together and figured out something, or perhaps he reckoned that Rad was just another trigger-happy saddle tramp, determined to kill him for some incident in the past which Pannard was unable to remember.

When a man led the sort of life that Pannard did, he inevitably made a host of enemies, had to surround himself with hired gunmen for his own protection, seek a place such as Lawless where there would be no lawmen on the run after him, where he could build up his own empire based on fear and greed, gather about him men such as himself. He thought of the girl, the way in which she had helped him the previous night when there had really been no reason for her to trust him, or defend him against those killers. He thought of her very steadily as he sat there in the growing heat of the sun, contemplating the glowing tip of his cigarette as he drew the smoke down into his lungs.

Meanwhile, in the house itself, Al Sullivan stood by the window, staring out into the dust-covered courtyard.

'That's the fella there's talk about, Ella?' he asked, softly. 'He could make bad trouble for you.'

She smiled with some show of indulgence. 'I know the sort of man he is,' she murmured. 'There's something in his past which is still hurting and he won't be able to think or act straight until he's got it out of himself.

Something to do with Pannard.'

'That figures.' He spoke soberly, eyed her with a fresh curiosity. 'But he's no man for you, Ella. He'll stay here and help you just so long as it suits him to do so, and then he'll ride on and leave you, just slip away. Wouldn't surprise me if he ain't got a price on his head in some state.'

'He isn't that sort of man, Al.'

'How do you know the kind of man he is? Now that your father is dead, you're ready to believe that Ed Pannard did it, and any stray *hombre* who comes riding in, looking for Pannard, threatening to hunt him down and kill him, has got your sympathy. You're too trusting.'

She studied him over a long and thoughtful interval, then shook her head. 'Now you're just being cynical, Al. You've lived with these men in Lawless for so long that you're beginning to think like them and look upon every man as a potential outlaw.'

'You're pretty blunt in these things when you've got your mind fixed on something, aren't you?' Al spoke with the easy way of long familiarity. 'But don't trust him too far, not until you're more sure of him than you can possibly be now. He may turn against you. Even if he doesn't, there's talk in town that Pannard is going to do all he can to finish this *hombre*.' As he spoke, he turned his gaze to the tall figure seated on top of the corral fence. 'I wonder what it was that happened between those two men. It sure must've been something pretty big for them to feel the way they do about each other.'

She stared at him, inwardly surprised at her cold and analytical study of him. She thought that she knew Sullivan. He had been her father's friend and had known her since she had been little more than knee high to a grasshopper. On several occasions he had given them sufficient warning of an attack which was to be made against them, and they had been able to fight it off. Now she relied on him even more than ever before to let her know what was happening in town.

'What is Pannard doing now?' she asked pointedly.

'He's getting men together. Soon they'll be riding with him. Whether they mean to ride this way or not, it's hard to tell. Sheriff Abbott is in with them, swearing the men in as a posse to make it all look legal.'

'Sheriff Abbott!' There was naked scorn in the girl's tone as she faced him squarely. 'He does nothing unless Pannard gives the order. That's the only way he can keep that job.'

'Sure.' Sullivan shrugged his shoulders, the flesh on his bony features drawn down on to his cheeks. 'But there's nobody else in town who'll take the chance of standing up against him, or Pannard.'

'If they decide to ride out this way, we'll be ready for them,' said the girl confidently.

'Pannard can call thirty or forty men to his back any time he likes,' said the other thinly. 'You can't fight off a bunch like that.'

She let out a long sigh, stood with her hands on the back of one of the chairs, her fingers hooked tightly around the polished wood, the knuckles standing out whitely under the skin with the pressure she was exerting. The stiffness on her face, the look of grim determination slipped a little. Deep inside, she knew that he spoke the truth. If Pannard did decide to use her act in shielding this man from his killers, to make an all-out attack on the ranch, then their chances of fighting off such an attack were slim indeed, were virtually non-existent.

Sullivan said, angrily: 'I don't want to see you throw all of this away, Ella, simply because of your feelings towards this man who just rode into the spread. So he came here to fight Pannard, and maybe he's one of the few men who would dare to stand up against him. But don't let yourself be drawn into this. If he has a quarrel with Pannard, let him sort it out himself and in his own way. Maybe he has nothing to lose. Your father fought for this place, built it up with his own hands, with the sweat of his brow. Don't throw it all away.'

She matched her will with his, faced him squarely, watched him so steadily that he finally grew impatient under her steady stare, looked away, glancing out of the window once more at Rad.

'I realize how you feel, Al,' she said finally. 'But this is my fight, too. Pannard killed my father, no matter what anyone says. Even if he didn't actually pull the trigger that killed him, he gave the order, and in my eyes that makes him just as much a murderer as the man who did the actual shooting. I want Ed Pannard dead, and I don't mind who does the killing.'

'You've grown suddenly hard, Ella,' Sullivan said, through his teeth. 'I don't like to see a woman this way.'

'Those men killed my father. If the world is ugly and bad, you have to be equally ugly and hard to fight it, otherwise you go under. There are men here who will take orders from me, do whatever I tell them to do. You've been around here long enough to know that to be a fact. And this man, Lobart, who rode in yesterday. I saved his life when Blanders and his crew were on his tail. Could be I can get him to do as I ask, too. He looks to be a handy man with a gun.'

Sullivan shook his head, a little wonderingly. 'I don't understand you at all,' he said harshly. 'You never used to be like this.' He was like a man out of his depth, not understanding what was happening. 'I don't think I like this.'

'You don't have to like it. Al,' she told him fiercely. 'I'm alone now, with my father gone, and I have to run this spread by myself. If I have to be hard, and sometimes cruel, to do it, then that's the way it will have to be.'

'Surely you must be aware of the difficulties facing a woman if she tries to do a man-size job like that?'

'I know it won't be easy, but life here

has never been easy, with those killers running the town, rustling our cattle, killing men when they sign on to work for me. I can read what's in your mind, Al. You're thinking that I'm all set to talk big, but that if the showdown comes, I'll have to back down without a fight. But you're wrong. I'll never give in to a man like Pannard — never!'

'All right, Ella, if you've made up your mind I don't reckon there's anything I can do or say that'll make you change it. I'll keep my eyes and ears open around town and let you know if anything happens.'

'That's all I want you to do. You don't have to fight with me, if you have no wish to do so.'

He watched her curiously for a few moments, then clapped the hat back on to his head and walked out of the parlour. She stood close to the window and watched him go, walking across the courtyard, long spurs raking up little spurts of dust behind him. He paused while still a few feet from Rad Lobart, made as if to say something to the other, then shrugged his shoulders, and walked over to the corral gate, whistled up his mount, climbed stiffly into the saddle, and took the hill trail without a single backward glance.

Going outside, she paused for a moment in the doorway, aware that Rad's gaze was on her, warmly appraising, knowing how she touched him. When a man rode long trails alone, almost any woman could strike a warmly responsive chord in him, she thought inwardly. That was how she struck this man who had ridden in the previous night, seeking her help, and the fact that she had given it so readily and without asking too many questions, ought to have put him in her debt. Maybe he had no wish to work for her, would prefer to ride on into Lawless at the first opportunity and have it out with this man, Pannard. But that was not what she wanted, and she knew sufficiently of herself, of her own mind, to realize that she intended to make him stay there.

Moving over to the corral, she motioned to Cal to bring out her horse and put a saddle on him. When it was done, she swung up into the saddle and sat looking coolly down at Rad. 'I want you to ride with me around the spread,' she said simply. 'There are some things we must talk about.'

He regarded her gravely for a moment, then slid from the top bar, brought out his mount. She waited until he was saddled up and waiting beside her, and then turned on to the hill trail.

Rad said nothing to her as they rode out of the courtyard and up on to the brow of the hill, past a wire fence which had been strung out alongside the trail, up beside a small creek that came bubbling, out of a well, cascading down the hillside in a series of leaps and bounds, the crystal clear water glittering brilliantly in the harsh sunlight.

There was a small herd of cattle browsing in the lush grass at the head of the long meadow, with a couple of men on horseback circling them watchfully. It was obvious to Rad that whatever had brought that man in from town, whatever news he had given to the girl, it had had a depressing effect on her, had clouded her mind. She seemed to be struggling inwardly with her thoughts, her eyes staring fixedly ahead of her, lips pressed closely together in a grimly determined line. They reached timber and then came on to a winding trail which led through the trees. There was the sharp, pleasant smell of the pines in the air here and a green coolness which contrasted with the heat outside the trees.

She sat easily in the saddle, swaying her body with every movement of the horse, evidently a born horsewoman. He watched her out of the corner of his eye, trying not to make it too obvious.

She was tall, he noticed, with a clear complexion, behind which the warm blood flowed richly, the long hair the colour of ripening corn in the sunlight, cascading over her shoulders. Her lips were red and clear, and her eyes dark, with a shining depth to them. A truly beautiful woman, he thought, with something deep within her that showed through on to her face and in her eyes whenever she was not thinking the deep thoughts which so obviously depressed her.

'The man who rode in,' he began softly. 'He come from Lawless?'

She turned her head as he spoke and contemplated him closely. Then she nodded as though she had just heard the question. 'Al Sullivan is an old friend of the family. He's been very useful to us at times in the past, warning us of any moves that are being made against us in town. More than once, Ed Pannard has tried to get his hands on the spread. Al can keep an eye on him, let us know what plans are being made in town.'

'But what he told you today has worried you?'

She went on, crossed a bare stretch of

ground, the sunlight shining on her hair under the wide-brimmed hat. She appeared to be debating within herself whether she dared confide in him or not. Then she seemed to reach a decision.

'Those men who came after you last night. They were some of Pannard's men. They know you're here but, with only a few of them, and because my men had rifles laid on them from three sides, they decided not to make any trouble. Al says that Pannard has given orders that you're to be taken from here by force. Sheriff Abbott is swearing in men for a posse to ride out with him and take you in. No doubt, to make it legal, they'll have some trumped up charge against you.'

'Then the sooner I leave here, the better. I don't want you to be involved in this. You've already done more than enough for me.'

She smiled at that, but there seemed to be no mirth nor warmth in her smile.

'You don't understand. Pannard sees

in this a way of killing two birds with the one stone. He gets you arrested or shot, and he takes over the ranch. If you ride out of here, that may solve the problem as far as you are concerned, but it won't help me.'

'What do you want me to do?' he asked directly. They had reached the summit of the narrow hill trail, and as if she had been anticipating his question, the girl stopped her mount abruptly. She pointed down below her. As far as the eye could see, the broad grasslands stretched away to the wide horizons, to where a wide river glistened faintly in the sunlight.

'All that land you can see, as far as the river, belongs to the Bar X spread. My father built it from nothing. When he came out here thirty years ago, there was only wilderness here, and they were just beginning to build Lawless and Silver Creek. People told him he was a fool trying to breed cattle here. If it wasn't the droughts, it was the Indians who raided every settlement that was put up in those days, but he somehow won through. Now that he's dead, I mean to keep it just as he left it. But I need men I can trust, men who are not afraid to use a gun and who won't run out on me just when things begin to get rough.'

'You're asking me to stay on here?' He tried to keep the incredulity out of his tone. 'But you know nothing about me. You don't know whether I'd run or throw in my lot with Pannard if it would save my skin, you don't know — '

'I know all I need to know about you,' she declared. 'I don't care what sort of a past a man has, whether he's bad or good, so long as he's a man and I can trust him implicitly. Unfortunately, such men are rare. I thought you were one, but perhaps I was mistaken.'

When he said nothing to that, she glanced at him sharply as though defying him to deny it. 'Will you stay?'

There was an almost pleading note to her voice now, an expression which made him turn and look directly at her. He saw her now as a woman, a little unsure of herself, knowing that she had to face up to problems which were almost beyond her.

'You may get your chance with Ed Pannard, if he's the man you came to kill.'

He thought about it for a long moment, lips pressed tightly together in a hard line. Then he nodded. 'I'll stay,' he said, 'but not for the reasons you've given.'

She smiled, seemed to relax. 'I don't mind about your reasons,' she told him. She sat square on the saddle now, without looking at him. 'You have to do whatever you think to be right. I won't ask you what this man did to you that makes you want to kill him. I only know what he did to me. That is enough for me to want him killed.'

'It won't be easy to find proof that he was behind the killing of your father. Do you want me to do that for you as well?'

'If you can,' she said, in a smaller voice. 'But I think I ought to tell you that one of my men tried to do that chore for me. They found him in the desert three days later. He wasn't a very pretty sight. They must have dry-gulched him, shot him in the back, three or four times and left him for the buzzards.'

'And you're afraid that the same sort of thing may happen to me?'

She gave him a keen glance, suddenly arrested by his remark. 'I wonder about you,' she said softly, 'whether you're as hard and as disillusioned as you try to make people think. I've only known you for a little while, but I've tried to make up my mind about you. Sullivan told me not to trust you, that you're the same kind of man as all of the other drifters who ride through the valley on their way into Lawless, a man on the jump, with the law at his back, afraid to look over his shoulder because of what he might find standing there, waiting to shoot him down in a street of some town. He told me that you'd be taking the trail over the hill if the going got really tough and Pannard and his men forced a showdown here.'

'Did you believe him?' It was a direct question, simply said. He saw from her face that whatever she may have thought of him earlier, she was trying to trust him, was trying to see behind the mask he had built up in front of him to hide the long bitterness that had grown in him over the long, weary years, the terrible judgments which he had formed on his fellow men. He knew himself that from the time when he had discovered about Pannard, life had ceased to be quite the same for him. Before that time, before he had even heard of this man's name, there had been a fresh mystery about every morning, and a glowing brightness in the heart of his camp fire whenever he had found himself at night on the wide trail, with the sky as his coverlet and a saddle or the soft grass as his pillow.

But as he thought of the well-thumbed book which reposed now in his saddle bag and of what had been written in it, he knew that life could never be like that again until he had come face to face with Pannard and had destroyed him utterly. There would be no more waking to a fine, dawn-brightening morning with the promise of warmth in the air and the leaves on the trees just budding into green. His camp fire, whenever he sat by it, would be dull and grey as ashes to his vision.

'I always form a first opinion of any men I mean to hire,' the girl said abruptly, her eyes flicking over him as if seeing him clearly for the first time, 'and I try to stay with my original decision.'

'And what might that have been as far as I'm concerned?'

'I don't think you're like the others. You may be drifting, but you have a purpose in it, and I doubt if it's because there's the law on your trail. But you do have something inside you, driving you on, something hard and devil-like, which you have to purge yourself of, before you can become a real man again.'

'You see a lot,' he said slowly. He had never met anyone who could read him in this way on so short an acquaintance before, and it disturbed him a little, particularly as it was a woman.

'Why?' she asked. 'Why are you this way? What did this man do to you that makes you want to kill him so badly?'

'I think you'd better not ask,' he said.

She shrugged her shoulders slightly. 'The vengeance trail is a long and hard one for any man to follow. My father did it for several years, ever since Pannard tried to take this spread away from us by any means he could. It killed my father in the end. Make sure that it doesn't do the same for you. There are evil forces at work in this territory and particularly in Lawless itself. I know enough about you to realize that sooner or later you'll want to ride into Lawless and try to force a showdown for yourself.'

'Does it matter to you how Pannard dies?' he asked abruptly.

She turned in the saddle to face him and, when she spoke, he noticed that she did not answer his direct question. 'Pannard is a powerful man. He has ways of having his orders carried out that we do not know of.' Her attention was focused thoughtfully on him. 'Don't do anything rash, I beg you. A bullet could come from any direction if you rode into Lawless seeking to kill Pannard like that. Believe me, my way is better.'

'To stay here and wait for them to come to you?' He shook his head very slowly. 'That is a way that could lead to disaster. If you want to fight men like this, you have to do so in your own way and attack them when they aren't expectin' it. Pannard has only to throw the whole weight of his force against you and it would be the end. There could only be one outcome of that, no matter how many guns you got to help you in the fight.'

'What does that mean?' she asked tightly.

'I'm goin' into Lawless tonight. Has it ever occurred to you that they may have corrupted this man, Sullivan, so that he gives you the wrong information? Even if he didn't do it willingly, they may have found out what he's been doin' and forced him to tell you wrong.'

'Not Al,' she said, but her tone implied that she was trying to convince herself and not him. 'He was with my father when they first came to this territory. He'd never throw in his lot with Pannard.'

'But you cannot be sure,' he persisted. 'If there is danger for you here, then you should know everythin' there is to know. I can find that out for you.'

Her face was tight as she retorted: 'But would you be alive to bring that information back from Lawless? Don't forget that Pannard seems to know as much about you as he does about me.

He had his men watch the stage trail for you, knew when you were leaving Silver Creek. He could have killed you there if he wanted to.'

As she spoke, she turned her mount, rode back into the timber trail. Rad followed close behind, thinking his own thoughts. He had not intended to ride out into Lawless that night until she had begun their conversation and, even now, he was not quite sure why he had said it, unless it was because of the deep-seated restlessness that kept bubbling up inside him, forcing the thoughts through his mind.

* * *

Rad left the Bar X ranch around nine o'clock that evening. He knew the girl was watching him from one of the windows, but he did not look round as he rode out, cutting across the dusty courtyard and upgrade into the timber-topped hills. There were clouds building up in the east now, tall thunderheads that lifted clear into the darkening sky, but to the west the sunset was a glory of bright reds and golds and greens, painting a glowing canvas across the horizon. The brilliant colours lay behind him and a cool wind blew against him as it sighed down from the enclosing hills which lay around the ranch in a wide circle.

Although he felt the urgent need to get into town and find out what he could about Ed Pannard, and the urgency was enough to bring on the restless side of his nature once more, he could not shake away the feeling of unease which threatened to dominate his mind to the exclusion of everything else; therefore he made a wide detour away from the main trail and rode up among the cool pines, where he could look down on to the trail and see any riders who might be on it.

Darkness came long before he reached Lawless. He had guessed that the town lay almost ten miles from the Bar X ranch, but it was soon obvious that it was more than fifteen miles into town. Shortly before he came within sight of the place, the moon lifted briefly, then drifted behind the gathering storm clouds and the first few drops of heavy rain began to patter on to his head as he circled around the town, edging off the main street, and cutting into the town along one of the inevitable winding alleys that led off the street. He rode slowly between small, slant-roofed houses and long, low warehouses and stores, windows broken or coated with dry dust. The rain came on in earnest while he was still some distance from the main street and, finding himself an empty place, he dismounted and moved the horse into it, out of the rain that was churning up the dust into mud.

Blending with the darkness, he moved out finally into the main street. Here there were yellow lights which bloomed out of open doorways and through half-open windows. The coming of the storm had brought only a slight cooling effect, and there was still a sticky, clammy heat in the streets.

He paused near the exit of the alley, rolled himself a smoke, standing with his shoulders against one of the wooden uprights. Lighting the cigarette, he drew the smoke down into his lungs and peered idly about him, careful not to attract any unwanted attention. A couple of men drifted out of the dimness, boots hammering hollowly on the boardwalk, passed him by with only a brief, cursory glance. His hat was pulled down over his forehead against the rain that dripped through the overhead woodwork, and he knew that even if these were some of Pannard's men, it was unlikely they would recognize him.

Two wide streets met at this point, forming a square in the middle of the town. At two of the four corners of the square were saloons, with the bank on the third and the offices of the town newspaper on the fourth. He concentrated his glance on this latter place, noticing that there was still a faint light showing in the wide windows, evidently coming from one of the back rooms. It was possible, he figured, that a man who ran the town newspaper would know most of what went on in the place, and he might be a fair-minded and honest man who was not in the pay of anybody, determined to keep the paper above such things. Rad had known one or two editors and they had all been honest men who tried to give their readers the truth, even though it could make them very unpopular in certain quarters. One man he had known had been killed because of this, although nobody had ever proved who had done it.

He tossed the half-smoked cigarette into the wet ground, ground it out with his heel, then stepped across the street to the newspaper office. The door was locked, but as he knocked loudly on the glass, he saw a door at the far side of the office open and a man's figure framed against the light. The other peered forward, then came over to the door and unlocked it, drawing back a chain which also secured it. Lawless was an uneasy town and a man like this, if he did happen to be honest and unafraid, would naturally take precautions.

'Yes?' asked the other in a thin, tired voice. 'Who is it? What do you want at this time of night? The office is closed and I'm getting the paper ready for tomorrow.'

'I'd like to talk to you if I may,' Rad said quietly. 'This is very important. It won't take up much of your time, and I can talk to you without interrupting your work.'

The other peered closely at him, shook his head a little as he said: 'I'm afraid I don't know you, do I?'

'No. I just rode into town. I'm working for Ella Redden.'

'For Ella?' There was a question in the tired voice. Then the other opened the door a little wider and stood to one side. 'Come inside. Don't stand there in

128

the doorway. You make a perfect target for anybody who might be watching in the shadows.'

'Sure is an uneasy town,' Rad said as he stepped inside.

The other closed the door behind him, locked it, slid the chain back into place and then pulled the shade down quickly and snapped it shut. Straightening, he said harshly:

'Why did you come to see me? Don't you know that it's dangerous for any of Ella's men to be in town right now?'

'I heard somethin' about that,' Rad confessed. He hitched the gunbelt up a little around his waist. 'Al Sullivan rode out to the ranch this mornin' with some news about what was goin' on in town.'

'Then you should have known enough to stay away.' There was no emotion in the other's voice. He led the way through into the back room where the press was being set up. A young boy, dressed in a blue smock, was in the room, checking the type and cleaning it.

'I don't know as much as I'd like to about Pannard,' Rad said tightly. There was something in his tone which made the other turn and look at him more closely. 'I only signed on for Ella Redden because it suited my plans.' He noticed how the other's eyes narrowed at that, and went on hastily: 'Don't get any ideas from that remark. I'm not workin' against her. But I came here for only one reason. To kill Pannard. I'm not interested in any other killers there are in Lawless, although I gather it's a place where most of these men hide out when they're on the run from the law. But it's Pannard I want.'

'So did a lot of men,' said the other sharply. He sank down in one of the chairs, stretched his long, thin legs out in front of him. 'But they're all dead now. He has an army of men in and around Lawless, knows every move that's made against him.' He broke off as the boy came forward across the room.

'That's all of the type finished, Mr

Ellis,' he said. 'Will you be wantin' me any more tonight?'

'No, Johnny. You'd better get home now. I'll see you again in the morning.'

'Yes, sir.'

The boy left the room with a sidelong glance at Rad. A moment later there was the sound of the chain being withdrawn and then the street door closing.

'Now, Mr — '

'Lobart. Rad Lobart.'

'Mr Lobart. How can I help you?'

'You can begin by telling me all you know about Ed Pannard.'

Ellis lit a cigarette, leaned back in the chair, his eyes hard. 'He came here about a year ago, as far as I can remember. Nobody knows where he was before he headed this way, although there was some talk that he worked in the east, made some money gambling in Silver Creek, then headed this way and bought one of the saloons, the Silver Dollar across the square. He seemed a little different from the usual type of man we got here ready to help anybody who got into difficulties and — '

'What sort of difficulties?'

'Oh, money usually. There might be a drought, or someone's well would inexplicably run dry and they needed money to tide them over.'

'But why didn't these people go to the bank if they needed a loan?'

'Sometimes a rancher is chary of going to a bank when he can get a loan from someone he believes is a friendly neighbour of his. But when the time came to collect and things were no better for them, he showed his true nature, took over their ranches, stock, everything. It was about that time, too, that Sheriff Cassell was shot in the back. Again there was no proof as to the identity of the murderer, although when Pannard put up his own man, Abbott, things pointed in one direction.'

'And now he owns most of the town?'

'That's right. He wanted Ella's father to sell out to him. He even went so far as to offer him a reasonable price for the spread, which shows how much he wanted it. But Redden refused to sell. He'd built that place himself and it was, I reckon, the only place he knew. Besides, his wife is buried there. She died a couple of years or so after Ella was born.'

'So Pannard tried to get it away from them by force?'

Ellis gave him a quizzical look. 'Again there was no direct proof. It started subtly with a few head of cattle being rustled off their range. The hill ranges were always looked on as providing fair game for rustlers. But gradually, as more and more of Redden's beef began disappearing, he hired more men to keep watch and gunfights broke out at night on the spread. Some of the rustlers were killed and there was circumstantial evidence to tie them in with men that Pannard was known to have on his payroll, but he maintained that if they were rustling cattle, then it was done without his knowledge and certainly without his connivance.'

'What do you know about Redden's death?' Rad asked.

'Very little. I was in here when they brought his body into town. Some cowpoke, riding through the hills, came across it, said he found a riderless horse and managed to catch it, and was leading it into town when he stumbled across this man in one of the creeks. Reckoned he must have been thrown by his horse and drowned, probably hitting his head on a stone on the creek bed. Then he went and examined him a little more closely, and what he found brought him hightailing it into Lawless, hunting for the sheriff. Abbott got a bunch of men together and they rode out to take a look-see and bring the body back. He'd been shot in the back, three or four times they reckoned, and at close range. Plenty of rocks just on the edge of the creek at that point and a gunman could have hidden there and dry-gulched him without much trouble.'

'But they never found out who did it?'

'No. Abbott started hunting around, asking questions. For a while they held the cowpoke who found the body, but there was no real evidence against him, and as they also found some money in Redden's pockets, robbery couldn't have been the motive, and this cowpoke had no other reason to kill him. Even if he did, it's unlikely he would have ridden hell for leather into town to report the killin' if he'd done it himself; more likely he'd have ridden for the border before anybody came along and found Redden. In the end they let him go, and that's where the matter ended.'

'Ella Redden feels sure that Pannard was behind the killing, even if he didn't actually pull the trigger of the gun that shot her father down.'

Ellis rubbed his chin thoughtfully. 'I'd go along with that,' he murmured, 'but if you're going to be in town for any length of time, I wouldn't tell that to anybody you don't know. Things have a way of getting back to Pannard and he would see to it that you didn't live long enough to start anything against him.'

'I've heard of the way Pannard makes sure nobody talks against him,' said Rad grimly. 'Could be he'll find it a little more difficult to keep me quiet. He tried once before, setting his men out on the trail from Silver Creek with orders to hold up the stage and take me off it.'

'Hold up the stage?' Ellis looked at him in surprise. Then he nodded his head slowly. 'Yes, I did hear something about that. Jake was talking in the saloon about some man who was taken off the stage after a bunch of outlaws had tried to attack the way station at Gunsight. So you're the *hombre* they took.'

'That's right. Fella named Clem Blanders and some other gunhawks. Kept me for a while in a shack up in the hills.'

'Then maybe you know what you're

up against.' The other got to his feet, moved over to the press, began to arrange the type on it, his back to Rad. 'That would make a good story for the paper, but I don't dare to print it. Certainly I couldn't link Pannard's name with the holdup.'

'I understand.' Rad gave a quick nod. He turned towards the door, then halted abruptly. Out of the corner of his eye he saw Ellis stiffen at the same moment, knew that the other had heard the same sound, the faint creaking of a wooden floorboard from the outer room. It was then that he remembered the boy who had left a little earlier. He had opened the street door, closing it but not locking it behind him. Someone had come inside and was at that very moment on the other side of the door, probably a gunman who had changed his position at that moment for a more commanding control of the doorway, ready to shoot down the first man who stepped through into the outer room.

Quickly, Rad motioned Ellis to

silence as the other moved away from the press. Slipping forward, easing one of the guns from his belt, he reached the door and pressed himself close to the wall on one side of it. He waited for a breathless minute for any fresh sound from the other side of the door, but heard nothing. Yet he was certain he had picked out something.

Behind him, Ellis tip-toed across the room to his desk on the far side, opened it cautiously and brought out a heavy revolver, checking the chambers quickly before he came over to stand beside Rad.

'All right, come on out!' Rad commanded in a loud voice. 'We know where you are and you're covered by two guns.'

His command brought no answer beyond the faint sound of the rain as it beat against the glass of the windows and the sound of a group of riders moving along the street. Perhaps the man had slipped back through the street door once he realized that his presence there had been discovered. On the other hand, it could have been the boy coming back for something he had forgotten, but if that was the case, why was he being so secretive? Surely he would have come into the room even though he knew they were there.

Reaching forward, Rad closed his fingers around the knob of the door, felt the blood pounding in his veins, his heart thudding against his ribs. For all he knew, the man might be standing right behind the door, his finger tight on the trigger of a gun, ready to blast him as soon as he pulled the door open and stepped through. On the other hand, he told himself that if there was a gunman there he was probably one of Pannard's men and if he could take the other alive, there were ways of making a man talk, even if he were of the stubborn type. This was a chance he might not get again for a long time.

Turning, he motioned Ellis to the other side of the door, indicated that he was going to open it and move through.

Standing tall and erect, Rad said harshly: 'All right, mister, you've had your chance. I'm coming through for you right now.'

He dropped swiftly to his knees as he finished speaking, jerked the door open and threw himself forward and to one side, his shoulders coming up hard against the wall just inside the outer room. In the darkness it was impossible at first to see anyone there. Then there came the sharp crash of a gunshot and the bullet ploughed into the wall within inches of his head, aimed too high as the gunman anticipated him to rush through in an upright position.

Rad swung himself sharply, twisting himself around like a cat, his finger tightening on the trigger. Out of the corner of his eye, he glimpsed the faint movement in the far corner of the room from where the flash of the gun had come, saw the man move forward, lifting the gun in his right hand again, levelling it this time on Rad's body. In that same instant Rad knew that he had made the mistake of not extinguishing the lamp in the room behind him before going through the doorway. Now he had the light at his back, outlining his body, making an excellent target for the killer. He snapped a quick shot at the other, knew he had missed as the man came forward again. Now the other was less than four feet from where Rad lay, so close that even in the dimness he was able to make out the vicious grin on the man's face, to recognize the other as the man who had brought the mount for him when he had been kept prisoner in the shack in the mountains. For a moment the shock of recognition caused him to delay pressing the trigger and the gunman got in one shot before Rad fired. He felt the stabbing burning pain in his shoulder that slammed him back against the wall. Through blurring vision he saw Smiley stagger as the bullet caught him high in the chest, pitching him backwards and sideways, teetering on his legs, legs which seemed unable to bear

141

his weight any longer.

Then the other collapsed heavily on to the floor, the gun clattering from his fingers. With an effort, Rad pushed himself upright into a sitting position, resting his back against the wall. His shoulder throbbed painfully and his left arm seemed to have gone limp, with no feeling whatever in it. He tried to move it, but failed.

Ellis came out of the rear room, went down on one knee beside the gunman, turned him over on to his back, looked into the wide, staring, sightless eyes, then said quietly: 'He's dead. You got him plumb centre.'

He came over to Rad, saw that there was blood on the other's shirt, dribbling between his fingers. 'But you're hit.'

'Just a flesh wound, I reckon,' Rad said through his teeth. 'Guess I was a little slow in getting off that last shot.'

'I'll get Doc Trencher to take a look at it,' said the other, rising to his feet. 'Here, lean on me and I'll help you into the other room. I guess I'd better let the Sheriff know, though I reckon he'll soon come running. Somebody will have heard those shots.'

Even as he spoke, there came a furious pounding on the street door and a moment later somebody tried the handle, found that it was unlocked, and came in. Rad saw the three men who rushed inside, then got slowly to his feet as Ellis slipped a hand under his right arm, easing him into the rear room, taking him over to the chair where Rad sank down gratefully, letting the air rush from his lungs in a loud exhalation, He realised he had been holding it almost from the moment he had been shot.'

'What's happening here, Clark?' asked one of the men, a short, portly figure dressed in a topcoat and sporting a gold watch and chain. 'We heard shooting and came running.'

'Some gunman tried to get in and hold up the place,' Ellis explained. 'We tackled him and there was some gun play.' He paused as one of the other men came forward, nodded his head slowly. 'Glad you're here, Doc. Better take a look at my friend here. Bullet in the shoulder, I reckon.'

Trencher was a tall, thin-faced individual, with deep-sunk eyes that seemed to bore into Rad, making him feel uncomfortable. He gently eased the blood-soaked shirt away from the lacerated flesh, told Ellis to move the lamp closer so that he might see properly, then examined the wound, nodding his head as he did so.

'You're lucky. Maybe just scraped the bone, but no more. I'll have to dig for it, I'm afraid.'

'Go ahead,' Rad said through clenched teeth. 'It's got to come out some time.'

'If you got any whiskey, Clark,' said Trencher meaningly, 'I reckon you could spare a little for him. This isn't going to be easy.'

'Whiskey? Oh, sure, sure.' Ellis got to his feet, went over to the cupboard in the far corner, came back with a glass and a bottle, poured a good measure into the glass and handed it to Rad. 'Throw it back,' he said quietly. 'Won't be too bad for you then.'

Rad drank the raw liquor down, coughed a little as it hit the back of his throat. But it made a warm spot in his stomach and there seemed to be a pleasant dizziness in his head now, as if the room was turning slowly about its axis, the walls receding and advancing with a monotonous regularity. But even with the whisky inside him, the pain in his shoulder as the other dug for the piece of lead inside him was almost more than he could bear. He felt the sweat pop out on his forehead and it was as if a red-hot branding iron was being thrust deep into his body, sending waves of agony lancing through his chest and back, threatening to split him in half. He shuddered and Trencher motioned to Ellis and one of the other men to come forward and hold him down on the low couch where they had made him lie.

It seemed an eternity before he heard an oddly metallic sound and Trencher's voice reached him through the haze of pain, seeming to come to him from a long way off. 'There it is. I'll just bandage it up now. You'll have a stiff shoulder and arm for a couple of days and you won't be able to use that arm for a week perhaps.'

Rad nodded numbly, felt the other strapping up his shoulder. Then he must have lost consciousness for a few moments, for when he came round another man had come into the room and was standing beside the couch. Rad squinted up at him but for a few moments nothing seemed to come into focus except for a brilliant gleam of metal reflecting the light from the lamp. He screwed up his eyes and furrowed his forehead in an attempt to see properly.

Then, slowly, his vision cleared. The shining spot of light resolved itself into a silver star pinned on the man's shirt and, above it, he made out the puffy features of a florid-faced man, long-nosed and narrow-eyed, who looked down at him with no expression of concern on his face, merely a grim tautness that he noticed immediately. It wasn't necessary for anybody to draw him a diagram, to know that this was Sheriff Abbott.

'They tell me you shot the man in the other room, mister,' he said thinly. His voice did not suit his features, being high-pitched, curiously squeaky. 'You ever see him before?'

Rad opened his mouth to tell where he had seen the other, then checked himself. 'Never seen him before,' he said huskily, aware of the throbbing in his head. 'We heard him moving around but when I told him to step out, he wouldn't. We figured then that he might have been there to make trouble, that he might have a gun on us. When I opened that door, he fired a shot at me.'

'You claimin' that he fired first?'

'That's right. You can ask Ellis here.

He was there all the time.'

'Mr Ellis can stay out of this for the time being,' snapped the other. 'I want to hear your version of the shootin'.'

'Well, you've just heard it.' Rad tried to lift his head but the painful ache behind his eyes was too much for him, and he sank back on to the couch.

'Better lie still for the time being,' said Doc Trencher from somewhere in the background. 'I'll give you somethin' in a little while that'll allow you to sleep.'

'Not before he answers my question,' put in Abbott. 'I'm the law around here, and a man has been killed through there. I want to get to the bottom of it — right now.'

'You tryin' to suggest that I shot him down in cold blood, Sheriff?' said Rad, through his teeth. 'If that's what you're sayin', I've got a witness here to testify that I didn't.'

'No need to talk like that,' said the other harshly, 'I've got a job to do here, and I don't need you to make it any more difficult than it already is.'

Abbott questioned him further for several more minutes and Rad answered as truthfully as he could without giving away the true purpose for his being in Lawless. Finally, Abbott nodded to himself, then moved away. He paused in the doorway, looked back at Ellis, and said harshly: 'I'll want to have a talk with you first thing in the morning, Clark. In the meantime, I'll arrange for the body to be taken down to the morgue.'

'You see how it is here,' muttered Ellis, after the others had left. 'He only partly believes what you said. Even then, he's determined to try to force the blame for that man's death on to you. Once they get you inside the jail, they will find a way of silencing you for good. Maybe a lynching party. Wouldn't be too difficult to do that, feed plenty of liquor to a crowd of the wild bunch, and they would soon bust you out of jail and string you up from the nearest tree. It's happened before and no one has been able to stop it.'

'That's why Abbott wants to see you in the morning, to force you to change your mind about any testimony you might give regarding the way it was when I shot that gunhawk?'

'Could be,' nodded the other. He stared down at his hands with a certain expression of helplessness on his face.

Rad tightened his lips. He tried to move his shoulder as he pushed himself higher on the couch. Things had taken an unexpected turn and, for the moment, he felt at a loss as to what to do for the best.

Ellis said harshly: 'In the past, whenever Pannard or Abbott wanted to make somebody change their minds about testimony like this, a man either knuckled under and did as he was told, or he found his store burned down, sometimes while he was inside. That way, they made sure he wasn't around to testify, anyway.'

'I see.' Rad tried to force the pain and weakness from his body. 'I guess the best thing I can do is get out of here tonight. That way, they won't be able to do anything to you, and if they want to hunt anybody down, it will have to be me.'

'Don't be a fool,' said the other, looking up sharply. 'You're in no condition to stir from here. Besides, I've been thinking. How did they know you were here? It's obvious they were after you, not me. As far as I see it, there's only one person who could have tipped them off about your presence here.'

'The boy who was working with you,' Rad said after a moment's thought. 'He was the only one, and he did slip off pretty quickly once I'd come. He'd have known that the street door would have been left open, too, in all probability.'

'And right now, it's my guess that Johnny is somewhere outside, watching this place. If he sees you leave, he'll let Abbott know within minutes.'

'Is there a back way out?'

'There is, but you've got no way of being sure it isn't watched, too.'

Rad made a sudden decision. 'That's a risk I'll have to take,' he said, thickly. 'Now help me up off this couch.'

For a moment the other merely stared down at him as though unable to believe his ears. Rad guessed that although an honest enough man, Clark Ellis was also concerned with the safety of his own skin, and inwardly the other would welcome Rad's removal from his office.

'You sure you know what you're doing?' asked Ellis in a faintly shaky tone. He got to his feet, bent and placed his arm under Rad's right shoulder, helping him to his feet. For a moment Rad swayed as the blood rushed pounding to his head, and his knees seemed turned to water. He would have fallen had not Ellis held him up, taking his weight against his side.

Gradually, taking great gulps of air down into his heaving lungs, Rad succeeded in forcing the weakness away to the extent that he was able to stand unaided on his feet. Slowly, his vision blurring every few seconds, he made his way after the other, into a small room at the very back of the building. It was in darkness and there was a musty smell in the air, sharp at the back of his nostrils. Boxes were strewn around on the floor, and he knocked his shins on them several times as he made his way across the room.

'This way.' Ellis's voice reached him from the darkness close at hand. A moment later he heard a key being turned softly in a lock, with a faint grating of metal on metal. Then a door opened directly in front of him, and a gust of cold, moist air rushed against him, chilling his body where the sweat had congealed on his back and forehead.

He went forward unsteadily, forcing the pain and weakness down. Whatever happened, he had to keep a tight hold on his buckling consciousness and not collapse, otherwise it could mean the end for him. He moved out of the building, peered about him through the slanting rain. Nothing moved and there was scarcely any sound there. He heard some harsh yells from the direction of the main street on the other side of the building and not far in front of him something scurried across the ground, vanished through a small hole in the wooden fencing a couple of yards away.

The rain fell full on his face, reviving him and, for the first time that night, he was glad of it. He took a step forward, put out his right hand to steady himself against the wall. Ellis's worried voice reached kim from the open doorway.

'You sure you can make it? You don't look too steady to me.'

'I'll be all right,' he said tautly. 'Once I get my bearings. I've got my mount stashed away in one of the empty warehouses down one of the alleys.'

'Good luck!' murmured the other.

A moment later, the door was shut and bolted after him. Forcing himself upright, he shuffled along the yards that ran the whole length of the rear of the building, his eye gradually becoming accustomed to the darkness so that he was able to step around the wooden boxes and piles of rubbish which littered the place. He struggled to orientate himself. The noise from the saloons in the main street could be clearly heard now and enabled him to pinpoint his position with a fair degree of accuracy. There was a narrow passage a little way off to his right, and he staggered towards it, reaching out for the low wall as he half fell. His head still hummed and throbbed, and it was difficult for him to keep upright. With every step he took his legs threatened to give way under him, to pitch him forward into that deep blackness of unconsciousness which had been hovering close to him since he had forced himself up off that couch.

There was no doubt that Ellis, in spite of his talk, had been glad to be rid of him. Everyone in town, it seemed was afraid of Pannard and the other killers who had taken over this town.

That made things very difficult as far as he was concerned. A lot would depend on getting someone to talk to him and help him; and with men afraid for their lives, that was not going to be easy.

Half-falling, he made his way along the dark passage, arms and legs hitting the low walls on either side. Gritting his teeth, he came out at the other end, found himself in the narrow alley where he had hidden his mount. Pausing, he glanced about him to obtain his directions, felt sure that the building which faced him was the one. Very cautiously, he edged towards it, watching the darker shadow which was the open doorway leading inside. Nothing moved there, and yet he had the unshakable feeling that some presence was there, waiting for him, some shape just inside the shadow, standing with a drawn gun, ready to fire at him the instant he showed himself.

He tried to throw off the feeling, telling himself fiercely that it was only his imagination, that anyone intent on watching the newspaper offices would be out front. He waited for a long moment as he reached the doorway, his body pressed tightly against the cold, rain-soaked wood of the wall. No sound from inside. That in itself sent a little warning thrill racing along his nerves. If this was, indeed, the place where he had left his mount only a little while before, then it should have been possible for him to pick out some slight movement there. He felt sure this was the place and, after a few moments, he edged around the corner of the door, his prying eyes searching through the darkly shadowed interior. At the far side he saw the loose piles of straw which had been pushed up against the wall, exactly as he had seen them before. There was no doubt at all that this was the place, *but there was no sign of his mount.*

He stood quite still for several seconds, feeling about him with his senses, alert and watchful for danger. Yet curiously, he found none. There was the faint smell of dragged-up dust in the air, as if somebody had been here recently. He looked to left and right, discovered nothing, but knew that someone had been here, found his mount, and taken it away.

In case there was somebody there, watching from the shadows, he set one foot down in front of the other, making the movement slow and easy. The floor was simply hard-packed earth, and as he moved his foot struck a tin can, sending it rattling a couple of inches across the floor. Small as the sound was, the echoes it made seemed to swell and bounce from one side of the warehouse to the other, increasing in volume every second. He stood quite still, his heart thudding painfully in his chest. The wound in his shoulder ached intolerably and the bandages which had been strapped around it seemed to be drawing more tightly around his body, as if shutting off his breath. A coolness ruffled the small hairs on the back of his neck, and in that same moment there was a brief movement somewhere in the darkness ahead of him, but higher than he was, and he guessed there were stairs somewhere leading up to a second storey. He stood rigid, then eased one of the guns from leather and lifted his head tautly, peering up into the blackness.

'All right,' he said softly, his voice carrying in the stillness. 'Step down out of there.'

He heard someone suck in a gust of wind and then let it out in slow pinches. A moment later the movement he had heard before was repeated, then he saw the shadowed figure coming down some steps leading up into a hayloft, which he had not noticed earlier. The man came forward until he was only a short distance from Rad, and in the faint light which filtered through the doorway, Rad felt a sudden shock as he recognized the other.

'What are you doin' here, Jake?' he said thickly. 'You nearly got your fool head shot off there. It could've been anybody skulking there in the shadows.'

'Just found myself a place to sleep,' said the bewhiskered stage driver. He chuckled dryly. 'Was it you brung that horse in here a while back?'

'That's right.' Rad nodded. 'You were hidin' there then?'

Jake gave him a sly glance. 'I've seen a lot tonight while I've been lyin' up there. There was some *hombre* came in only a little while after you'd gone out, just before I heard the shootin' close by. I reckoned it was you when he took the horse, but I guess it couldn't have been.'

'It wasn't,' Rad said tightly. He holstered the gun. 'But you haven't answered my question. What are you doin' hiding in here? I figured you'd be takin' that stage back to Silver Creek.'

'So I would've, but there was trouble when we got to Lawless after what happened on the trail. Seems Pannard figured we might have recognized some of those men who held up the stage and took you off it, so he tried to stop us

160

from talkin'. I don't know what happened to those three passengers we carried into Lawless. I figure they may be dead by now. I got out of the depot by the rear exit and I've been hidin' out in town ever since. I had you figured for one of his men when you came in just then, that's why I kept so goshdarned quiet. Didn't want to risk gettin' a bullet.'

His glance strayed to the bandages around Rad's left shoulder and the thick, bushy brows went up a little. 'What's happened to you? Did those *hombres* do that when they took you off into the hills?'

Rad shook his head. 'I managed to get away from them,' he said tightly. 'I got myself a job on a spread just east of here. Seems this girl who runs it after her father was killed reckoned that Pannard is at the back of his murder and is also tryin' to rustle off her cattle. She wanted an extra gun to help fight him off.'

'It'll need an army to fight Pannard,'

said the oldster soberly. 'He can call more gunmen to his back than any of the ranchers in these parts.'

'So I reckoned. That's why I came into Lawless tonight to see how things were shapin' here. I had a talk with Ellis, the editor of the local paper. He knew a little, but before he could tell me everything he knows, we had a visitor. It was one of the men who was in that gang which held up the stage, although he came in later, bringing up a horse for me when they took me back to town. I had to shoot him down. Got a slug in my shoulder for my trouble.'

'Doesn't look the sort of wound for a man to be wanderin' around town at this time of night with,' grunted the other.

'You're right. But the sheriff they have here seemed anxious to pin something on me. I pulled out of Ellis's place. He's scared of Abbott and Pannard, and I reckon he would have turned me over to the sheriff rather than run the risk of having the newspaper office burnt down about his ears, as has happened in the past with those who don't co-operate with Pannard.'

4

Hideout in Lawless

Jake looked up at Rad with a break of fresh interest on his face. He nodded his head slowly, 'That makes sense, I reckon,' he admitted, thoughtfully. 'But now that they have your horse, what do you intend to do next?'

Rad shrugged. 'Seems they want me to stay around in Lawless for a while,' he murmured. 'Guess I'll oblige 'em.'

'You could be gamblin' with your life,' said the other. He stepped across to the door and peered cautiously out, glancing up and down the narrow alley. Then he came back, stood close to Rad. 'You won't be able to do any shootin' with that hand, anyway. Guess you need a place to hole up for a while.'

'Do you know of any such place in town?'

'Place I used to visit whenever I was on a run here, but I didn't go there tonight just in case they knew about it and was watchin' the house.'

'It's more likely that Pannard is interested in me, not you. Think we could make it there without being seen on the way?'

'I guess so.' Jake gave a brief nod. 'It ain't too far from here. You sure you can make it in your condition? You don't look too steady on your feet at the moment.'

'I'll make out all right,' Rad told him through tightly gritted teeth. 'Just lead the way and try not to make any noise. There could be eyes watchin' every inch of town.'

'That's a smart way to figure it,' agreed the other. He moved towards the door again, slipped out into the night, feet padding on the beaten earth. Rad followed, keeping close on the other's heels. There was still plenty of yelling and raucous singing from the saloons in the main street, but Jake led him in the opposite direction, over towards the outskirts of town, where there were few lights and nearly every place was either abandoned or in utter darkness.

Silence hung like a shroud over this part of town. A stray dog ran across an open patch of ground, vanished into the shadows. Rad jerked his head around at the sudden sound, then forced himself to relax. The cold night air, coupled with the rain that soaked his clothing so that it clung to his skin, served to keep him awake and even made him feel a little better than when he had staggered out of the newspaper office.

Jake led the way through a maze of twisting alleys, each seeming to be darker than the last, before pausing in front of a low building, set a little distance from the others, standing alone in a wide patch of ground. There was a faint chink of yellow lampglow showing around the edge of the shutters over the window, and Jake paused to glance intently in all directions before slipping forward towards the door. He rapped gently on it, waited.

Rad moved close to him, shivering a little in his wet clothing. He suddenly felt sick and weak, his head beginning to spin. There was the sound of shuffling footsteps at the other side of the door, then a voice called: 'Who is it?'

'Me — Jake. Open up, Carl.'

There was a brief pause, then the rattle of a chain and the door swung open. Rad had a vision of the old man who stood there holding the lamp high over his head as he peered out into the night.

'Come on inside, Jake. We heard about the stage bein' held up. Figured you'd be out this way before now.'

Rad ducked his head as he passed through the low doorway, followed the others into the small parlour. The man placed the lantern on the small table, gave Rad a bright stare, brows raised in an inquiring line as he turned his head and looked at Jake.

'This is a friend of mine, Carl,' Jake said, jerking a thumb at Rad. 'He was on the stage I brought in from Silver Creek, only a bunch of outlaws held us up this side of Gunsight and took him off at gunpoint. He managed to get away from 'em and got taken on by Miss Redden. There was a little gunplay over at the newspaper office a while back and he caught a slug in the shoulder, but not before he took Smiley with him.'

'You shot Smiley Williams?' said Carl incredulously. 'He was one of Pannard's slickest gunmen. Ed won't like that. Believe me, mister, your life ain't goin' to be worth a plugged nickel once he hears about this.'

'I figure he already knows,' Rad said sombrely. He lowered himself gratefully into one of the chairs at the table. 'Sheriff Abbott was there on the scene within minutes of the shooting. He tried to make out that I was in the wrong. Ellis reckoned he'd do all he could to get me inside the jail on some charge, and once that happened, there would be a lynching party formed by tomorrow night and I'd be swingin' from some nearby tree.'

'He wasn't far wrong at that,' said Carl grimly. 'But you're welcome to stay here until that shoulder of yours heals.'

'Thanks.'

Rad felt wet and tired and, beyond that, lay something else which he did not understand, a feeling of something half-done, an unpleasant feeling which he tried in vain to throw off.

'Figure you could get us a bite to eat, Carl?' asked Jake, sitting down in the chair opposite Rad. 'Been a while since I had a bite of cooked food.'

'Sure, sure.' The other tossed a handful of wood on to the fire that glowed feebly in the hearth, waited until it had blazed up, then went through into a room at the back. 'Ham and eggs do?' he called through to them.

'Be better than anythin',' Jake

answered. He looked at Rad. 'Then you'd better get some sleep. You'll feel more like a man in the morning.'

He ate the bacon and eggs slowly, chewing on each bite, washed it down with coffee. It should have brought some of the feeling back to his body, but it did not, and there was only the vague emptiness which he did not understand and, going into the room where a bed was waiting for him in the corner, he felt dried out and useless, like a warped board that had been left lying too long in the sun until all of the strength had been burned out of it and it was no good for anything any more.

Sinking down on to the bed, he tried to reach out in his mind for the old, carefree days before this thing had come upon him, before he had found out the truth about so many things he had earlier been prepared to accept at their face value. Even as he thought upon those days, the weight of his anger and bitterness settled deeper upon his soul and he turned over on to his good side to face the wall, determined to surrender his weary body to the deep-rooted tiredness which was waiting to claim him, so that he would not have to go on thinking these black thoughts any longer.

Sleep came almost at once to him, and when he woke there was the first pale light of dawn filtering in through the small window, and he lifted himself up with an effort. His shoulder still ached and there was a stiffness in it which made it difficult for him to move his arm. The doctor had said it would take a few days to heal sufficiently for him to be able to use it, and he felt more useless than ever before. He knew that Ella Redden might be wondering what had happened to him since he had refused to heed her warning about riding into Lawless alone. Maybe she would believe him dead, just another man killed in the long fight to destroy Ed Pannard and everything for which he stood.

But he knew there was a great risk if

he tried to slip out of town in his present weakened condition. He might be spotted within minutes of leaving this place.

A moment later there was a knock on the door and Jake came in. He grinned across at Rad. 'You look as if you slept plenty good,' he said. 'How's the shoulder now?'

'Still pretty stiff, but I guess that'll wear off soon.' Rad looked out of the window into the backwork of alleys and passages that ran among low-roofed buildings on which the grey dawn shone wetly. There had been plenty of rain through the night, but the clouds were now beginning to break up and drift away, leaving patches of dark blue through which the last of the stars shone faintly as the dawn brightened in the east. There was a solid net of lines across his forehead as he wrinkled it in sudden thought.

'Any more trouble durin' the night?' he asked.

'None that I know of. You figure

there might have been?'

'Just thought that Pannard might have been scouring the town, looking for me once he found I'd slipped away from the newspaper offices. I don't doubt that Abbott told him as soon as he left Ellis's.'

'Leave things as they are,' counselled the other. 'There's breakfast waiting downstairs.'

They went down and ate the food which the old man had prepared. As they ate, Carl said slyly: 'There was some ruckus during the morning, about three hours ago. Lots of comings and goings in the alleys. I reckon it must've been Pannard's men out lookin' for you.' He stared directly at Rad as he spoke, his eyes bright and sharp. 'You got any idea why he should want you that bad?'

'I figure he knows why I'm in town, that I've come here to finish some business, and when the showdown comes, only one of us is goin' to walk away from it.'

'So that's the way of it. Can't say you surprise me by that. A lot of men have ridden into Lawless lookin for Pannard's hide. But he's still alive and they ain't.'

'Like I've told Rad, Pannard don't scare easily,' put in Jake. He rubbed his mouth with the back of his hand.

'I figure he might feel more scared if he knew why I'm here, just who I am,' Rad said enigmatically.

Carl grinned. 'I guess that even if you was Billy the Kid, he wouldn't be too scared, not in Lawless. He's got too many men out, too many ears listening to what's going on. Any man who rides into town is watched from the minute he arrives to the moment he leaves.'

Rad remembered the youth in the printing room at the newspaper office, perhaps the one person he would never have suspected, and he knew that the other told nothing more than the truth. It was impossible to say who was watching and relaying information back to Pannard. The man sat like some vile spider in the centre of a vast net spread throughout the town of Lawless, getting news from a score of sources.

Finishing the breakfast, Rad got a razor from Carl, some shaving soap and hot water, and succeeded in shaving himself with one hand in front of the small mirror tacked to the kitchen wall. He stood by the window for a moment as he dried his face on the rough towel, watching the first wave of sunlight as it broke over the edge of the hills in the far distance, seemed to hang for a moment on the crests, and then shatter into a million pieces that came splashing across the intervening plain towards the outskirts of town, touching the houses nearby and finally flooding in through the window and touching his face as he stood there with his eyes screwed up a little. Just for a moment, a little of the good feeling came back into his veins, but after that the recent recollections came and took the feeling away, leaving the bitterness behind.

The Silver Dollar saloon was getting its first customers as Ed Pannard walked up on to the boardwalk, paused for a moment to stare around at the square, basking in the warm sunlight, with steam rising from the rain-soaked ground, hanging like a faint mist over the streets as all of the moisture was sucked avidly from the ground, the heat of the sun already beginning to bake it hard, forming cracks over the smooth surface.

He did not wait long, but turned abruptly on his heel, pushed open the doors with the flat of his hand and stepped through into the coolness of the saloon. The bartender noticed him at once, seemed to have been on the look out for him, knowing almost to the second when he would be coming. Seating himself at one of the tables, away from the door but close to the window where he could see almost all of the way along the street, he waited until the bartender brought the whiskey bottle and a glass over to him.

'Any sign of Abbott this morning?' he asked tightly.

The bartender shook his head. 'He hasn't been in all morning, Mr Pannard.'

'Send one of the men out to fetch him. Tell him I want to see him here in a hurry.'

'Yes, Mr Pannard.' The other backed away, spoke to one of the men at a nearby table. The man glanced hurriedly over his shoulder in the direction of the blackcoated man pouring a drink from the whiskey bottle, then scraped back his chair, left his drink untouched on the table, and moved quickly out into the street. Pannard did not glance up to see whether or not the man had gone to carry out his order. In this town, he knew that men obeyed every command he gave without question.

Abbott was inside the saloon within five minutes, his flabby face perspiring as he stood in front of Pannard.

'You wanted to see me, Mr Pannard?' he said in a low tone.

'That's right, Sheriff.' Pannard nodded towards the chair opposite him. 'Sit down and listen to what I have to say.'

Abbott lowered his huge bulk into the chair, sat forward so that he seemed to be overflowing it. He waited patiently for Pannard to speak, looking oddly uncomfortable as if he knew, without asking, that he was in some kind of trouble.

'This man who got away from Clem and the others and who seems to have signed on to work for Ella Redden. You're sure that was him in the newspaper office last night?'

Abbott swallowed thickly, his Adam's apple bobbing up and down nervously in his throat. 'I never saw the man before, but Clem maintains it was the same man. I wouldn't have thought he'd have had the nerve to ride into Lawless, not after what happened.'

'That is the trouble with you,

178

Abbott,' said Pannard, sarcasm in his booming voice. 'You don't stop to think. Maybe he figured that this would be the last place where we would think of looking for him. Maybe he wants to find out more about what's happening here.'

'But why should he be here in the first place?' asked the other. 'He doesn't look like one of the usual type who come drifting into Lawless. If he was, I could understand it.'

'I want you to find him, no matter how you do it. I want him before sundown today. He's here for some reason and he could be dangerous.'

'With a slug in his shoulder?' said the other, surprised. 'If you want my opinion, he'll be in bed for a week at least. Which means he's holed up some place. There can't be many who will shelter him if they know you want him brought in.'

'You reckon that was his horse you found in that abandoned warehouse?'

Abbot shrugged. 'Must've been. He

probably put it there so he could grab it without any delay if there was trouble.'

'Then he's got to be some place in town, and whoever is hidin' him will know who he is. I'm warnin' you, Abbott, I want him brought in before sundown, but I want him alive.'

'That may not be so easy.' The other's tongue ran swiftly over his dry lips and he glanced meaningly at the bottle on the table in front of him.

Pannard saw the other's glance, said with a faint sneer to his tone: 'Go ahead and take a drink then, Abbott, if you need it to steady your nerves.'

'It ain't that, Mr Pannard,' said the other, huskily. 'But I've heard about this *hombre*. Smiley was no mean hand with a gun, fast and deadly. I've seen him outshoot most of the men in these parts. But this *hombre* gunned him down while he was propped against the wall, firing into darkness as well.'

'If you're scared of Lobart, I figure I can always get myself another lawman to do your job for you,' said Pannard, his voice very soft. 'But then you'd be of no further use to me, and you know what happens to men who outlive their usefulness.'

The look on Abbott's face, the way the sweat began to run in tiny rivulets down his cheek, dripping from his brows, was enough to tell Pannard that the other understood the implications behind the lightly veiled threat.

'I'll bring him in,' said Abbott throatily. He reached for the bottle, nodding to the bartender to bring him another glass. The whiskey spilled on to the table as his fingers shook when he poured the liquor into his glass, and his hand was still trembling as he lifted the glass to his parched lips and downed the drink in a single gulp. Pannard eyed him closely, face twisted into a grimace of disgust.

Abbott poured a second drink, stared down at the golden liquid as he swirled it around the glass. 'I've been thinkin' about Lobart,' he said, hoarsely. 'He must've slipped away from the newspaper offices by the back way. I had the boy watching the front entrance and he never came out there. Could be that I can get Ellis to talk.'

'He'll know nothing,' Pannard said thinly. He sipped his drink and lit a thin black cheroot, blowing smoke into the air. 'Lobart is no fool. He'll have guessed what kind of man Ellis is, and he'll have told him nothing.'

'Then he must have gone back to the warehouse, looking for his mount. When he didn't find it there, he'd get to thinkin' things out and he'd probably reach the conclusion that we'd got there before him and found it.'

'Then where would he go?' Pannard's lips stretched thin and very tight. 'He doesn't know this town. He wouldn't dare to ask around for shelter, so it figures that he must've met up with somebody who does know the town.'

Pannard paused as he drew deeply on his cheroot, the tip glowing red. 'Somebody who probably knew him by sight, if not by name.'

'Reckon that ought to narrow it down a little,' Abbott agreed. He seemed to have steadied himself a little now that Pannard was more interested in working out what could have happened to Lobart than in concerning himself with the fact that he had slipped through Abbott's fingers the previous night.

'Who's likely to know him in town? Only Ellis and he wouldn't dare help him.'

Abbott drew his brows together into a straight line of concentration. He said finally: 'Could be that one of those men who was on the stage with him when it left Silver Creek might have met up with him.'

Pannard jerked up his head, stared at the other for a few moments, then nodded his head rapidly. 'Of course. We scattered that bunch when they arrived here, but if I recollect rightly, there was a Pinkerton man, and that ranch owner, but he was moving on west, and I reckon he'll have pulled out long ago.

Nothing to keep him in Lawless.'

'So that narrows it down still further.' Abbott finished his drink, sat back in his chair. 'You figure it might have been Jake? He knows his way around town far better than any of the coach passengers would and he ain't got no likin' for us. Reckon he'd help this hombre, just to get back at us.'

Pannard nodded, thought of that slowly, his mind reaching out and around the whole thing. Abbott saw the truth of the situation come to the other in slow stages, saw it form around his mouth and darken his expression. 'You know where Jake shacks up whenever he comes into town?'

'Sure thing,' nodded Abbott quickly.

'Then get some of the boys together and go out there. If Lobart is hidin' out there, I want you to bring him in. Remember, I want him alive. There are some things I want to know before he dies.'

Abbott nodded, pushed back his chair and got heavily to his feet. He gave the bartender a quick nod and then went out, the swing doors closing behind him.

Through the window, Pannard watched the other as he waddled across to the sheriff's office and went inside. For a long moment Pannard sat lost in thought. He had the feeling that there was something more to the desire of this man to ride into Lawless and kill him, more than mere vengeance. There had been men before who had ridden in with the intention of killing him and they had all ended up the same way, buried six feet down in the clay on Boot Hill. But this man was somehow different. He could not recollect the other's name, it rang no responsive bell in his memory of past events as the names of most of the others had.

He ran over in his mind all that had happened during the past years which could possibly account for this private feud against him, and found nothing.

Sunlight flooded over the town beyond the window. The sun had almost reached its zenith and shadows were small and narrow in the street. The harsh glare touched the blistered paint on the wooden walls of the buildings, shone on the whorled surface of the dust that lay deep in the street where the hoofs of many horses had kicked it into a meaningless pattern of hollows and ridges. On the far side of the square, a mangy dog lay in the dust, striving to find a cool spot in the shadows, panting slightly, its tongue lolling from its mouth. It moved a little as he watched, heaving itself up on to its forelegs, too uncomfortable now that the sunlight was beginning to move around the corner of the building, bringing the heat with it. Slowly, it dragged itself a few feet back into the alley, sank down again, its head between its paws.

Abbott came out of the sheriff's office a moment later, buckling his gunbelt around his monstrous middle. Pannard felt a sense of grim amusement. The other did not look the part of a lawman, and he doubted very much if Abbott would ever put himself into a position where he had to face up to a gunman. He was a frightened man, whose only use was that he could take orders without questioning them and there were times when he had flashes of inspiration, such as when he had suggested those men on the coach as having possibly helped Lobart to find a place to hide in Lawless.

Abbott moved over to the other saloon on the opposite corner of the square, pushed his way half through the doors, his back to Pannard. A few seconds later he backed out and a group of men came through the doors from the saloon, moved over to where their mounts were tied to the hitching rail in front of the building. They mounted up and rode off, followed by Abbott.

The dust lifted by their mounts hung like an orange-yellow cloud in the still air, settling slowly. Gradually the sound of the pounding hoofs faded into the distance and silence crowded on to the street once again.

Pannard flicked the grey ash from his cheroot. For a moment he felt pleased with himself. Once he had Lobart in his hands, he would find out the answers to a lot of questions which had been troubling him ever since he had heard of this man in Silver Creek.

★ ★ ★

Rad was seated in the chair at the table in the small parlour when Carl came rushing in, breathless. Over by the door of the bedroom, Jake glanced up, startled.

'What's all the hurry, Carl?' he asked thickly.

'Trouble,' said the other jerkily. 'Abbott and a bunch of men are headed this way. Spotted 'em a couple of minutes ago.'

'You sure of that?' asked Rad harshly, getting quickly to his feet.

'Sure as June rain. That outfit there is

all spragged up for trouble. I reckon they've guessed you're here, or maybe they've had somebody watchin' the place after all.'

Rad removed his gun from the right holster, broke the gate and spun the cylinder gently. Then he slid the weapon back into leather again and walked to the window.

Carl was watching him narrowly during this performance. He said tightly: 'You ain't figurin' on takin' 'em from here, are you? You'd never have a chance. Once they surrounded the place, it would only be a matter of time. Even if you killed off most of 'em, they could bring up plenty more men.'

'You have a better idea? I don't see any horses around and we wouldn't stand a chance on foot.'

Carl looked about him tensely. Then he shook his head. 'I'll back you if you like,' he muttered.

Rad thought fast. 'Maybe there won't be any need for that,' he said quickly. 'If you could hold 'em off for a couple of minutes, I figure I can grab myself a horse and give 'em the slip.'

'How?' asked Jake, mystified.

'If they wanted to come in from the rear, could they do it?' Rad asked, ignoring Jake and turning to Carl.

'Not if they wanted to ride in. They can only bring their horses up to the front of the place. Reckon they'll do that and then swing around on foot. Plenty of cover out there.'

'That's what I figured.' Rad gave a quick nod. He made for the back of the house. 'Just wait until they dismount and then open fire. Give me a couple of minutes.'

'What'll you be doin'?' asked Jake.

'Grabbin' off one of their mounts. I figure they'll leave 'em there at the front of the building in that alley. They'll figure I'm still in here, specially if you open fire on 'em. By the time they realize I'm not here, it'll be too late. I reckon I can draw 'em off before they do too much damage here.'

'Good luck,' called Jake as he slipped

through the small store room at the back of the building, out into the yard. He pushed through the pile of rubbish which cluttered the place, through a gate at the far side which hung crazily on broken hinges, and out through a narrow passage which in places was so narrow that he could barely force his way through it.

In the distance he heard the approach of a bunch of riders, kept his head well down as he heard a harsh yell, clearly echoing among the houses. Immediately afterward a gun shouted, the hard racket bouncing from one building to the next, dying away in slowly atrophying echoes. Clawing the gun from its holster, he edged forward. He was afraid that the sudden movement might have opened the wound, started it to bleed again, but there was no time to bother with that now. He reached the end of the low fence which had afforded him cover, risked a quick glance around it, then drew his head back quickly. The nearest of the men was only ten feet away from where he was crouched, guarding the milling horses. The rest of the men had spread themselves out, were moving rapidly to encircle the house.

Rad had picked out Abbott's voice from somewhere in the background, yelling orders, and a moment later the sheriff's voice yelled: 'If you're in there, Lobart, you'd better come out with your hands lifted, or we'll come in and get you out.'

Jake called something from the house and punctuated his remark with a shot that brought a cry of pain from one of the men crouching down behind the wall. A volley of fire crashed against the building and Rad gritted his teeth as he shifted position, edging towards the man who stood with the horses, his back towards Rad now as he watched the fire-fight with interest. The horses milled furiously at the sound of the gunfire and the man was having all of his work cut out to keep them calmed.

Abbott called something more, then yelled to his men to pour more fire into the place.

From somewhere came the splintering crash of glass as a slug smashed it to pieces, and Rad took advantage of this to move forward until he was standing right behind the man watching the horses, the gun reversed in his right hand.

For a split second, as though he had somehow sensed Rad's presence at his back, the man began to turn, his head twisting, his mouth beginning to open in a soundless yell as he saw the gunbutt descending on the back of his unprotected head. It struck with a sickening thud, and the man's knees gave under him. A voice, anonymous and unlocated, yelled: 'Back here, Abbott.'

Without pause, Rad swung himself up into the saddle of the nearest horse, kicked at it with his spurs, urging it forward. At the same time, he fired the Colt close to the rest of the horses, stampeding them along the narrow alley.

The man who had yelled the warning came rushing out from behind the fence, his gun lifted as he strove to line it up on Rad's chest. He ran right into the path of the running horses and Rad saw him go down with a wild yell of fear welling up from the depths of his throat as flailing hoofs struck him viciously, kicking him to the earth. A flurry of shots came after Rad as he raced the horse along the alley in the direction of the main street. A quick glance over his shoulder showed him the rest of the men, with the ponderous figure of the sheriff, piling out of the passage. A wild shot ricocheted off the wall of one of the buildings, then he was out in the main street, hauling on the reins to bring the horse around.

The confusion behind him grew greater as he pushed the horse to the limit, spurring along the street. He was aware of men rushing from the saloons, of faces pressed against the windows, peering out at him as he rode by. A couple of shots came sighing along the street at his back, hummed close by his head as he ducked low in the saddle. Then he was out of town, with the last of the buildings drifting by him.

Dust formed a silver screen around him as he headed for the hills. He knew that pursuit would not be long delayed. He had slipped through Pannard's men by the skin of his teeth and they would not rest until they had ridden him down and caught up with him. Once he got to the Bar X ranch, there might be safety for him. He felt sure that Pannard did not want to risk a showdown there at the moment, not until he had brought more of his men together and was more sure of himself. There were still plenty of folk in the valley who remembered the girl's father, Rad reasoned, as he gave the horse its head, and it was unlikely that they would stand idly by while Pannard attacked the ranch.

It was more than ten minutes since

he had left town, and he was perhaps two miles away, leading his mount up a narrow, winding ravine that led into the thick timber, when he saw the riders spurring out of town in the distance behind him. It had been an extremely valuable ten minutes as far as Rad was concerned. It had given him a precious start on the others, and although he knew that his dust would give them enough to go on so that they would be able to trail him, even though he tried to throw them off, it meant he had a good chance of outrunning them to the ranch.

His shoulder was throbbing painfully now and there was fresh blood on the bandages wrapped tightly around it. His left arm felt numb all the way down and there was little feeling left in his fingers whenever he tried to clench them, to force life back into them. At the top of the slope he paused, then pushed the animal forward. It crashed headlong through the saplings which barred his path, sliding, thrusting down occasionally on to its haunches, buffeting the trunks of the taller trees that lay in its path and, at times, he was almost driven from the saddle by low branches which whipped across him as they plunged through them.

Gritting his teeth, he somehow managed to hang on to the saddlehorn with his good hand, and he felt that if he could maintain his lead over the posse that was following him until he came out of the timber, the horse would outrun all of the others which were after him. It was tired now; he could sense that by the way it stumbled at times, swerving around the corners of the narrow, half-seen trail through the trees, but it was of good stock and he reckoned it could gallop faster and further than an ordinary horse if it was really pushed, as it was being pushed now. He rowelled the spurs deep into its flanks, sorry for the way he was having to treat it, but knowing that he had to keep well ahead of Abbott and his men if he was to stay alive.

They came down from the hill trail and on to the broad mesa, cutting on to the wider trail in a series of hurtling, bounding strides that carried them swiftly forward into the heat of the early afternoon. Rad sat well forward in the saddle now to give the horse its best chance of outdistancing the pursuers. He caught the faint sound of a high-pitched yell, half-muffled among the trees, and thought he heard the crashing of horses through the under-brush. Once or twice the horse stumbled and Rad felt the blood pounding through his temples when-ever this happened, knowing that if the horse fell it could snap its foreleg cleanly in two.

But they were over the mesa within five minutes, heading for the regular trail, linking up with it as it swung over the desert to the north. He had been banking on Abbott and his men not taking this trail. It would have led them by a roundabout route, for the trail over the hills was far shorter than the normal route, but they might have made better time along it.

Glancing back over his shoulder, he saw the first rider break cover from the trees, pause to glance out over the stretching flatness of the mesa, then point a hand as the others came out on his tail. He reckoned that if anything he had increased his lead slightly, and the thought gave him added encouragement as he spurred the horse forward. There were still several miles to travel before he hit the perimeter of the Bar X ranchlands, but if he could stay ahead of these men and not run into trouble, he ought to make it all right.

This was the way of it for the rest of the long afternoon. It was nearly five o'clock when he turned the horse through a clump of catsclaw and heeled it into a narrow ravine that led down to the East Meadow of the Bar X spread. He knew there was a small line camp here with maybe three men keeping a watch along this stretch of the wire. Not enough men to keep off Abbott and his bunch if he decided to push his luck and move in to arrest Rad. No doubt Abbott would be able to think up some trumped up charge to make things sound legal and give him an excuse for moving on to Bar X land.

He stayed with the trail, moving downgrade, and it brought him presently on to the grassland where a small herd was grazing peaceably, the two cowboys riding herd on them, circling the cattle slowly. In the heat of the late afternoon, everything seemed oddly peaceful as he rode down towards the camp. One of the men, who had been left at the fire to prepare the evening meal, glanced up as he rode into camp, gave him a friendly nod.

'You headin' back to the ranch house,' he said, getting to his feet. 'Better stop for a bite. Be ready in five minutes.'

'Sorry,' said Rad, remaining in the saddle. He was aware of the other's curious glance on the bandages round his shoulder. 'But there's trouble followin' close on my trail. Abbott and a bunch of his men.'

'Ain't you the hombre who signed on with Miss Ella a couple of days ago?' queried the other.

'That's right.' Rad looked longingly at the pot sizzling over the fire and the can of coffee bubbling away on its hook, the smell rich and appetizing in the still air. He would have given anything to have been able to get down and accept the other's invite. But it was more than his life was worth to do that, he told himself fiercely, Abbott would be spurring his men on, hoping to overtake him before he hit the ranch.

'What's Abbott on your trail for?'

'Reckon it's Pannard who wants me,' Rad said simply, saw by the look on the other's face that the man understood what he meant. 'They tried to buck me in Lawless, but I managed to get one of their horses and stampede the rest. I suppose he could take me in on a charge of horse stealin'.'

'You want us to say you haven't ridden through here when they come?' asked the other meaningly.

Rad considered that for a moment, then shrugged, 'Won't make much difference. They can't be more'n ten minutes behind me. They know which way I'm headed. All I can do now is try to stay ahead of them until I hit the ranch house.'

'Sure.'

The other continued to watch him as he gigged his mount away from the camp fire, circled around the herd and cut across the wide meadow. Twenty minutes' travel took him up over the lee of the hill in the distance on the far side of the wide valley, and when he paused atop the crest and peered back, he made out the tightly-bunched group of riders, still doggedly following him, but now they had shortened the intervening distance, were gaining on him slowly but surely.

He had made a mistake in pausing to talk with the man at the line camp. He should have continued to ride, he told himself, as he turned in the saddle. On the far side of the hill the land roughened and he rode through narrow, high-walled fissures in the rock, into a deep ravine with a gravelled bed along which he rode carefully. There was a shallow basin at the bottom of the ravine and a pool of clear water in it. In spite of the nearness of his pursuers, he paused to give his mount a drink and a chance to blow. It stood hipshot almost at once.

Moving up through the ravines and fissures, around gigantic boulders which almost blocked their path, he came at last into the open, level ground and made out the ranch house in front of him, less than a mile distant.

He was almost falling from the saddle by the time he rode into the small courtyard. He heard the door of the house open, saw the girl come out on to the porch, then run towards him, shouting to two of the men who lounged near the bunkhouse. Then he was being led into the house, his senses spinning, his shoulder burning like fire under the tight, blood-sodden bandages.

5

Range Trouble

A long time seemed to go by and then Rad came back to consciousness to find himself lying on the couch in the parlour of the ranch, and someone was bathing his face with a damp cloth, wiping the sweat and dust from his features. He struggled up into a sitting position, found himself staring into Ella Redden's face. Beyond her he saw one of the other hired hands standing by the window looking out, his legs braced well apart.

'What happened to you, Rad?' asked the girl in a low, hushed voice. 'Your shoulder!'

He licked his dry lips, then felt the coolness of a cup placed against them, and swallowed the cold water gratefully, letting it slide down his parched throat.

'Never mind about that right now,' he said tightly. 'How long have I been unconscious?'

'Only a few minutes. Bill and I managed to get you inside. You collapsed as soon as we got you out of the saddle. I was trying to get some of the dirt from your face when you came round. I guess it was the cold water that did it.'

'Only a few minutes.' With an effort, he forced himself to his feet, swinging his legs to the floor in spite of the girl's attempts to keep him down on the couch. Unsteadily, the blood pounding through his head, he staggered to the window, standing beside Bill. The sunlight fell over the low hills in the distance and he could just make out the dust cloud that marked the position of the men who had pursued him all the way through the long afternoon.

Bill spoke quietly, evenly: 'Those men on your tail?'

'That's right. It's Sheriff Abbott and some of Pannard's hired gunmen. They cornered me with Jake, the stage driver, this morning, but I managed to slip away after grabbing off one of their horses. Pannard must've sent them after me.'

'What happened in town?' persisted Ella Redden, coming forward. She seemed to be more concerned about him than the men who were heading towards the ranch.

'I tried to have a word with Ellis, the editor of the local paper, but we were interrupted. I had to shoot one of Pannard's men when he attacked us.'

'I warned you about trouble if you rode into Lawless, but you wouldn't listen to me.' There was no emotion in the girl's voice. She moved to the window and glanced out at the approaching riders. Then she said sharply: 'Warn the rest of the boys, Bill. Tell them to stay out of sight until I give the word. I think I know how to handle Abbott.'

'He means business this time,' warned Rad. 'He's been told to get me and, if he values his life, he won't dare to go back to Pannard and admit that I got away.'

'We'll see about that.' She turned as the other man hesitated by the window. 'Hurry and do as I say, Bill,' she snapped. As she spoke, she went through into the other room, came back with a Winchester, broke it open and thrust a couple of shells into place, snapping it shut again.

Instinctively, Rad thumbed home shells into the chambers of his own gun. From the window he watched as the posse rode into the courtyard and reined their mounts in front of the corral. Sheriff Abbott moved his mount forward a few paces, paused in front of the door.

'I'm going out to him,' said the girl tightly. She moved to the door before Rad could make a move to stop her. Throwing open the door, she stepped on to the porch, the rifle held firmly in her hands.

'What do you want here, Sheriff?' she

called loudly, her voice clear. There was a faint beat of sarcasm in the way she stressed the last word. 'I thought your jurisdiction extended only to Lawless.'

'Now you don't want any trouble, Miss Redden,' said the other loudly. 'I'm here for only one reason, to bring in a horse-thief. That man you're hidin' stole a horse while he was in Lawless, rode him out here. We followed him all this way, so we know he's inside. Just you hand him over to us and we'll be ridin' back to town without any more trouble.'

'And if I say that you're lying, Abbott?'

From the window, Rad saw the Sheriff jerk upright in his saddle at that remark, saw his fingers clench tightly on the saddle horn, knuckles standing out whitely under the flesh. A dull red flush suffused his flabby features and his eyes narrowed until they almost vanished in the deep folds of flesh.

'You're bein' mighty foolish,' he said tightly. 'I've brought these men with me to help take Lobart in for trial. He'll get a fair hearin'.'

'You don't expect me to believe that, do you?' Ella lifted the Winchester slightly so that it was pointed directly at the other, her finger on the trigger. 'From what he told me, somebody stole his mount and tried to shoot him up while he was talking to Ellis, the paper editor. Somebody called Smiley. He's one of Ed Pannard's men, and I can see some others in this posse you've brought out with you. Now I reckon you'd better ride on out of here and take the trail back into Lawless.'

Abbott tightened his lips, sat upright in the saddle, trying to browbeat the girl as he laid his glance on her. 'You're asking for big trouble,' he said shortly. 'I don't want to have to look for him by force, but I will if you make me.'

Ella shook her head. 'I wouldn't try anything like that, Abbott,' she warned. 'I can kill you before you can make a move and my men are watching you from all around the courtyard, with guns laid on you from all sides. I've only to say the word and they'll open fire.'

'Now see here — ' began the other thickly, blustering.

'No. You listen to me. Do you think I can't see through your little scheme. Rad Lobart is working for me. I hired him a couple of days ago. I know that Ed Pannard wants him killed and that he sent you and these men out here to do just that. Now I'll give you exactly two minutes to move out, or my men start shooting.'

Near the window, Rad edged forward a little so that he could watch the men in the courtyard. There was a faint movement near the barn and he spotted two of Ella's hands waiting in the shadows. For a long moment it seemed that Abbott was going to risk a fight and call the girl's bluff, although Rad was not quite sure that it was bluff on her part. From what he knew of her, she was quite capable of carrying out her threat and ordering her men to fire on the posse.

Then Abbott wheeled his mount with an angry gesture. He shouted harshly: 'You'll regret this, Ella. It won't do you any good to resist the law, as you'll soon discover. All right, men, let's ride on out. The next time we come we'll be shooting.'

Rad let his breath go in small pinches through his nostrils, his shoulders slumping fractionally with relief. The girl remained on the porch looking after Abbott and the posse as they rode off, and a moment later Rad went out to join her.

'Seems to me you've just made an enemy of Abbott,' he said softly.

She lowered the rifle and turned towards him. There was a faint smile on her lips. 'He's no lawman,' she said quietly. 'He just carries out Pannard's orders, does his dirty work for him. He's a coward deep inside; he wouldn't dare to have ridden out here without those killers at his back.'

'I thought they intended to try

somethin' even with your men watching.'

She shook her head slowly. 'These men don't fight unless they have every advantage. They're more adept at shooting men in the back than facing them in fair fight.' She made a gesture with her hands, with her shoulders. 'It's beginning to get cold,' she murmured. 'Let's go inside.'

She turned and stepped inside. Rad paused for a moment, looked out over the courtyard and noticed that the men who had been waiting in the shadows had withdrawn, were no longer in sight.

* * *

Rad had a bunk fixed up for himself in the bunkhouse on the edge of the courtyard. That night, as he lay under the blankets, listening to the quiet sounds of the night and the even breathing of the other men with him, he turned over events of the past couple of days in his mind. He did not doubt that

Pannard would make a further play for him once he found out that he had got to the ranch in safety and that Abbott had been unable to get him off the spread and back to Lawless. But the question remained: how would Pannard do it? He might try to raid the place in force, bringing the full weight of his hired gunslingers to bear on the ranch, or he might try to get a man close enough to him, to shoot him in the back. There seemed to be a host of ways by which he could be killed. As yet, he did not think that Pannard knew the real purpose of his vengeance, nor why he was determined to kill him. If he once suspected that, Pannard would certainly act very differently from the way he was acting now.

He listened to the sounds of the horses in the corral, wondered if the girl was all right, alone in that ranch house. He felt a feeling of warmth go through him as he recalled the way in which she had stood out against Abbott and those gunhawks, as if daring them to start any trouble. She had a strong, firm jaw for a woman, he mused. But at times her face would soften and a hint of sadness would come to it, altering the shape of her lips and bringing a wistful look to her eyes. It was not good that a girl should have to run a big place like this, particularly when there were dangerous and unscrupulous men such as Pannard casting envious eyes on it.

He rolled over on to his side, watched the play of moonlight as it filtered through the window near his bunk, then closed his eyes and composed himself for sleep.

In the morning he had breakfast in the house with Ella Redden. For some odd reason, she had come to look upon him as different from most of the other hired men about the place, and he ate at her table, an honour reserved only for himself and Bill, the foreman.

Bill glanced at Rad across the table. He said shortly: 'We lost another thirty head of cattle a couple of nights ago, from the North stretch. Rustled during the night. The men say they saw and heard nothing.'

'You figure they may be lyin'?' Rad asked, feeling that this remark had been addressed more to him than to the girl.

'Could be. Seems strange to me that so many cattle could be herded off the range without one of the men noticin' something wrong. Unless they was all asleep, and they claim they weren't.'

'I'd like you to take a ride on up there, Rad,' the girl said, looking directly at him. 'If you think you're up to it with that shoulder of yours? They may try again, particularly if they think they can get away with it once more.'

'How many men are at the North camp?' Rad drained his cup of coffee, held it out as the girl poured him another.

'Five,' answered Ella Redden softly. 'All good men, been here since my father came. I thought I could trust all of them. Now I'm not so sure.'

'Could be that one or more of them is in Pannard's pay,' explained Bill. 'If they figured that nothin' would stop him taking over the place, they might be looking out for their jobs and this could be one way of making sure they keep them if Pannard does take over.'

'What makes you think these rustlers will try again at the same place? Seems more logical to me that they'd switch their attack.'

The girl paused on the edge of her answer. She watched him closely for a moment, then filled her cup from the coffee pot on the stove. 'You forget that they can keep a close watch over the range, and on every move that we make. They will know if we send more men to the North spread, or whether we decide to build up our forces at any of the other camps where the cattle are. When they see that nobody is being sent to the north pasture, they may decide to attack once again.'

Rad said: 'I'll drift down there and lend a hand and keep my eyes open for any trouble.'

Half an hour later he saddled up his

horse, swung up into the saddle. His shoulder was still stiff, but he had removed most of the bandages, although the girl had tried to dissuade him, and now he was able to move it a little more freely than before. He kept flexing his fingers, trying to work some of the feeling and strength back into them, lifting the gun from its holster and lining it up in front of him, forcing his muscles to obey his will. As he sat there in the saddle, he noticed that the girl had come out on to the wide porch and was watching him closely, a curious look on her face. She stepped down into the courtyard, moved towards him and stood beside him, her hand resting on the bridle.

'Take care of yourself, Rad,' she said softly, and he noticed the delicate colouring of her face as she tilted her head back to stare up at him.

'Believe me, I mean to do just that,' he said quietly. 'I've still got that score to settle with Pannard.'

He paused for a moment longer,

then, as she stepped back a pace from his horse, wheeled it around and rode out of the courtyard, taking the narrow trail that led north of the ranch house. Here it ran through a series of small meadows, well watered, filled with lush green grass. He did not hurry, knowing that he would reach the camp before nightfall, and not sure whether this trail was being watched by any of Pannard's men. He did not want to make it too obvious where he was headed.

Noon found him resting by a small stream that flowed through tall rocks and then splashed into a deep pool before meandering across the prairie. He hobbled his mount close to the water and made noon camp under a tall tree, lying out in the shade. The heat of the sun was a heavy pressure and he lay back with his hat tipped over his eyes, legs stretched out in front of him. For the moment he was grateful for the rest and the chance to forget about thinking things out, content just to lie there, soaking in the warmth and the utter stillness.

Slowly the sunlight moved around the side of the trees and he woke as it shone full in his face. Stretching, he yawned, peering about him. Judging from the shadow of the tree, he had been asleep for two hours or more. Time to be hitting the trail once more. He got to his feet, unhobbled the horse, let it have a further drink from the pool, then mounted up.

At the first convenient spot he left the uplands and cut down into the broad valley that led due north. After two hours of travel, he reached the far end of the valley, and the trail began to climb once more, leading him up to the undulating ridges that he had noticed on the skyline earlier in the afternoon. Then they had shimmered in the heat haze, purple and vague. Now that he had reached them, he noticed that he was in the tall grass again, guessed he had reached the southern end of the north pasture. He kept his eyes open for the first sign of the line camp.

The trail wound over the rise and fall of the crests of hills, skirting the pasture, and he wished he had cut straight over the grass rather than following the trail along what was proving to be a roundabout route. Fifteen minutes later he was glad that he had taken to the trail. Reining up his mount, he peered down from the saddle. The prints in the dirt were recent and something had hurried the men here for they held a deeper bite into the dried dust. He could tell at once that the prints had been made while the dirt was wet and that could only mean during the rainstorm which had happened on the night he had ridden into Lawless, the night Bill had said the cattle had been stolen from this pasture. He edged his mount forward slowly, a few steps at a time, keeping his eyes on the trail, and soon came across what he had been looking for: the unmistakable sign of cattle having been driven off along this trail. They had swung up from the grass which lay to his left, up across the trail at this point and through the rocky pass into the hills. From there it would be quite a simple matter to drive them out of the Bar X spread and to some place where Pannard could keep them until he had built up a sufficient number to take them to the railhead for transport to the east.

By that time, of course, their brands would have been changed and there would be nothing to connect the beef with the Bar X spread. All very clever and ingenious. The only question which remained to be answered now was how they had managed to do this without being seen by the men who were supposed to be guarding this herd.

He had his mind entirely on this problem and it was still with him a little while later as he rounded a bend and pulled up sharply at the loud bark of a rifle from almost directly ahead of him and not very far away.

The sound of the single shot had

been as clear and as sharp as the crack of a whip cutting across the silence. Halting the bay, he leaned forward cautiously in his saddle, searching the valley below and the rocks ahead of him for any sign of a tell-tale puff of smoke, but he could see nothing. Then, down below him, perhaps three hundred yards away, he saw the riderless horse plunging forward through the tall grass and, a short distance behind it, the figure of a man lying prone on the ground, his arms outstretched, fingers clawed in the last desperate attempt to fight off death which was inevitable.

The man's horse galloped on for a short distance, reins trailing, and then stopped, bending its head, eating the grass. Carefully, Rad eased the Colt from its holster and kneed his mount forward. Whoever had shot that man down there had been hiding close to the trail, and although he was, at the moment, well screened from that stretch of the trail, he knew that as soon as he rounded the sharp corner in front of him, he would come into full view of the killer.

He sat and waited, then heard the rattle of stones bouncing down the steep slope as a mounted man rode off at break-neck speed.

Acting on impulse, he urged his horse forward, throwing caution to the winds as he rounded the corner, cast his glance upwards until he saw the back of the rider on a narrow trail above him, headed away, spurring his mount forward at a cruel pace. There was no chance of catching him. Rad recognized that at once. Turning off the trail, he rode down amid a shower of stones and rocks on to the grass below, slid from the saddle on the run as he came alongside the sprawled body of the man.

A couple of zopilote buzzards, hovering in the vicinity, rose with a sharp sound of beating wings and clawed for the heavens, frightened away by his sudden arrival. But he knew they would not go far, would watch until he went away.

Gently he turned the man over, saw that he was still alive, but only just. His breathing was harsh and shallow, bursting up from his torn lungs, and there were flecks of blood on his lips and dribbling down his chin. His eyes opened, stared up at Rad without any sign of recognition in them. He seemed to be only half aware that someone was there.

'You got any idea who did this?' Rad asked tightly. He bent low to catch any words the other might utter, knowing that the man was fading fast, that the big, long sleep was nearly on him.

He saw the other's lips move as he tried to get words out, to force them past his teeth, saw the muscles of his scrawny throat cord and contract as he tried to say something.

'Bla-Blanders. He'd been . . . trailin' me all afternoon.'

The words were harsh and jerky, faint dry whispers of sound which Rad only just managed to catch as he held his ear close to the dying man's lips.

'Clem Blanders?'

A brief nod of the other's head affirmed this. Then he gave a sort of soft sigh and his head fell to one side, the eyes suddenly losing all of their life and clouding over. Gently, Rad lowered his head to the ground, stood up and looked about him.

Clem Blanders, one of Pannard's right-hand men. He ought to have known from the start that it would have been a coyote like that who would have dry-gulched a man and shot him in the back.

The killer would be miles away by now, he decided; and a quick glance at the buzzards whirling in sweeping circles against the lowering sun made him pause and then search around for some implement with which he could dig a crude grave for this man. It was either that or carry him on his horse to the line camp and bury him there. It took him the best part of half an hour to dig a grave in the soft earth.

Straightening his back when it was finished, he stared down in silence at the raised mound. By rights, he ought to say a few words over this grave of a man he did not even know, but he could think of nothing. Religion had meant very little to him throughout these long years and, turning on his heel, he made his way back to where his horse was standing patiently by the side of the trail. His shoulder was aching from the strain of digging that grave, but there was no fresh bleeding.

An hour later, just as the red disc of the sun was drifting down behind the skyline, he spotted the line camp directly ahead of him and rode towards it at a fast gallop. He was anxious to reach the end of his trail; he felt hungry and tired and the long ride through this country had not brought the sense of well-being and contentment which he had hoped it would when he had set off from the ranch that morning. There was a fire burning and a couple of Conestoga wagons drawn up close to it, the red, flickering light touching the canvas with a pale glow. He made out the shapes of three men squatting around the fire, and the smell of cooking beef and hot coffee came out of the still air to meet him as he rode up into the camp.

The herd was being bedded down for the night on the slope of a nearby hill. The lazy crooning of the cowboys circling it could just be heard in the distance. He rode on until he was less than ten yards from the fire, reined up and sat easy in the saddle, feeling the eyes of the men on him. Could one of these men be the dry-gulcher who had shot down that man he had found along the trail? he wondered tensely, letting his gaze flick from one man to the other. These were, he knew, hard men, working at a hard trade. They were men who had to be hard to keep alive.

One of the men got abruptly to his feet, stepped forward. 'You just ridin' by, mister, or are you here on business, lookin' for a job?'

'Neither,' said Rad easily, swinging down from the saddle. He went forward. 'I've been sent out here to help you boys. Miss Redden reckons that those rustlers might try for this herd again, seein' as how they got away with it a couple of nights ago.'

'You workin' for her?' asked the man tightly, still unconvinced.

'That's right. 'The name's Lobart. Rad Lobart.'

The other nodded slowly, then gestured towards the fire. 'Better sit down and get you somethin' to eat. You must've ridden most of the day.'

Rad turned his mount in with the others, squatted near the fire, feeling the warmth come out and envelop him. It relaxed him and he felt his muscles loosen after the long hours on the trail. The cook came forward and slapped more beef into the frying-pan, put more coffee on to boil.

Seated beside him, the tall, black-bearded man said: 'My handle's

Meekin. These are Slim Goodman and Walt Carrico.'

Rad nodded to the others, sat back on his haunches as a plate was handed to him, heaped high with strips of beef and potatoes. A mug of steaming coffee was placed beside him. He ate and drank gratefully, some of the warmth returning to his body. Not until he had finished and the plate was rubbed clean did he look up, watching Meekin closely.

'There was a shooting back on the trail,' he said slowly, quietly, his words falling into the deep stillness. 'Saw the man shot by some *hombre* hiding along the trail. The killer had too good a start on me to catch him, but the man spoke a little before he died. Claimed it was a man named Blanders who had been trailin' him all afternoon and who must've shot him down from cover.'

He caught the look which flashed between Meekin and the other men, a guarded expression which told him these men knew plenty about the killing. But it seemed they were still uncertain of him, still suspicious.

'You say you found this man along the trail, witnessed the shootin'?' said Carrico tightly. He stared at Rad across the blazing fire. 'What was he like?'

'Tall, thin-faced, greying hair at the temples.' Rad tried to recall anything more about the murdered man's features, then shook his head. 'That's about all I remember of him. I dug him a grave to keep the buzzards off him. It's back there a piece if you want to find it at any time.'

There was silence over the camp as he spoke, silence except for the snap and crackle of the flames as they bit their way along the dry wood which had been heaped on to the fire. Silence, except for the low murmur of one of the steers. Then Meekin said harshly: 'Sounds to me like Anderson.'

'One of your men?' Rad inquired.

'That's right. He's been with us for a couple of months now. Drifted into the camp one night and asked if there was any work. We were a bit short-handed at the time and let him stay on. He seemed a good man around cattle, and we never had any trouble with him.'

'Then what was he doin' along the trail?'

'He was supposed to be ridin' back to the ranch,' put in Carrico. 'You see, he wasn't on the regular payroll. We just let him have the job for a while to see how he fitted in here. Seemed he was a good enough hand, so we sent him along to the ranch to square things up with Miss Redden.'

'And on the way there, he was followed by Blanders and shot down before he could get to the ranch,' mused Rad.

There was something about that shooting which he didn't quite understand, something that didn't tie in. He himself didn't like it when a man was shot in the back by a bushwhacker, but if Clem Blanders had been tailin' Anderson before shooting him, it could only have been because he wanted to make certain it was the man he was after and to choose the best place for such a killing. Yet even so, he had the feeling that there was something more to it than that, that he was missing a bet somewhere here.

Darkness covered the world, crowding in from the far horizons that lay on the very edge of vision, with the sky overhead sharpened by the myriad pinpoints of light.

'You find anythin' else back on the trail?' asked Meekin pointedly.

Red paused, then nodded. 'Found where some cattle had been driven across the trail quite recently and then up into the hills. At a guess, I'd say there had been maybe thirty or forty head, although it was difficult to be sure.'

'You reckon that's where they took the cattle they rustled from here?'

'Seems highly likely. They were moved across the trail when the ground was wet, and the last rain was two nights ago. That was when those cattle were taken.'

'You could be right,' mused the other. He stared forward into the fire, rubbed his beard with his fingers. 'Did Miss Redden say anythin' to you about the rustling?'

'Such as what?'

'Such as why we never saw or heard anything? She must have some ideas about that.'

'If she has, she never mentioned them to me.' Rad held out the mug and Carrico poured him more coffee. 'But it could be that those rustlers had some help when they ran off that beef.'

Meekin jerked his head up sharply at this remark and his eyes narrowed to mere slits. 'What do you mean by that, Lobart?' he said thinly. 'You suggestin' that any of us were in on that deal with those coyotes?'

'Not you. But doesn't it strike you as strange that Anderson should have been shot on the trail by one of Pannard's men?'

'How do you know that Blanders is one of Pannard's men?' said the other narrowly.

'I know a lot about Ed Pannard,' Rad said soberly. 'Perhaps more than any other man alive. I came here for only one purpose, to kill him. Sooner or later I'll do just that.'

There was a new look on Meekin's face now. He regarded Rad with a little more concern, a look with awe blended with surprise. Then he shrugged his shoulders, made a little movement with his right hand.

'You think that Anderson was workin' in cahoots with Pannard?'

'Looks that way to me. If he was, then he could have talked and Pannard wouldn't have liked that. So he sent Blanders along to watch the camp and make sure that as soon as Anderson got separated from the rest of you, he was to make certain that Anderson never talked again. They could also have known I was headin' out this way, and they wanted Anderson dead before I could start askin' him any questions. They couldn't be sure that he wouldn't crack.'

'So they killed him,' murmured Carrico flatly. He stared at Rad unblinkingly over the rim of his mug. 'And you reckon they'll try to run more beef off the range from this herd?'

'I'm pretty sure of it.'

'If they do, we'll be ready for 'em,' growled Carrico. He rolled himself a cigarette, fired it and puffed the smoke out in front of him.

'You mean that you hope you will,' Rad said grimly. He lit himself a cigarette, lighting it with a glowing ember from the fire. 'They're cunning, these *hombres*, and they'll have had this camp watched carefully for long enough. There's no doubt they'll know exactly how many men you have here, as well as how many head of beef.'

Later that night, with the two other men having ridden in, Rad rode out with Meekin to check the sleeping herd. Both guided their mounts past the litter of gear on the edge of the fireglow, out into the deep darkness that lay beyond. The night seemed absolutely still and black, with only the faint shimmer of starlight to pick out the irregular shadow of the herd some two miles distant.

'How many head do you have here?' Rad asked.

'Nearly four thousand. This is a pretty big spread. Old Matt Redden left quite a place to his daughter when he died.'

'Don't you mean when he was murdered?'

'Waal, I reckon that's so.' The other's voice was edged a little with tension and it was almost as if he did not want to talk about the shooting of Ella Redden's father. 'Be that as it is, she's a very wealthy young woman, and I can see her point in wantin' to hold on to it.'

'Is there any reason why she shouldn't, apart from Pannard?'

'I guess not. But ain't Pannard

enough trouble for anybody to have? He's the biggest man around these parts, owns four or five smaller ranches himself, those that he got for virtually nothing after he closed down on the mortgages of the folk who couldn't pay back the money he loaned them.'

'Yeah, I heard about that. Seems an underhand way to get a hold of these places.'

'Weren't nothin' anybody could do about it. He had a lawyer come over from Silver Creek to draw up the new deeds, make sure they was all legal. Then he put this *hombre* Abbott into the post of sheriff, and that was that, I guess.'

'Wasn't there anyone who tried to stand up to him at that time?'

'Nobody that I heard tell of,' muttered the other.

They reached the herd and began to circle it slowly, letting their mounts have their heads, picking their own pace.

'Even if anybody had been stupid

238

enough to try,' said Meekin, 'he wouldn't have lived long in Lawless. Pannard would've seen to that in no uncertain manner. I've seen it happen. Fella named Holton. Wouldn't sell out to Pannard. He wasn't one of those who'd accepted a loan, independent sort of cuss. Pannard sent some of his boys to pay him a visit. He held 'em off as long as he could. Then they fired the barn and the wind carried the flames over to the house. They deliberately kept up a steady fire to prevent him from gettin' out and he died in the flames.'

'Guess he ain't liked in these parts.'

'There are those who ride with him, back up his play. Hired gunmen who drift in over the mountains, runnin' from the law, lookin' for a safe place to hide. He gives 'em safety in return for their guns. It might be that if we had some Government troops in the area like they had a few years back along the Kansas border, we might get some action and run him out of the territory.

But that ain't likely to happen. Not yet awhile, anyway.'

They rode around the huge herd, now bedded down for the night, with one beast occasionally stirring here and there with the inexplicable ways of these animals. Certainly it provided a tempting prize for any band of rustlers, riding in over the low hills, bunching some of these steers together, herding them away from the main group and galloping them across the plains to the south, where they would cross the main trail and drive them up into the hills.

And once in there, Rad guessed, there would be a multitude of trails where they would be led and it would prove virtually impossible for them to be located before the brands had been changed and they were ready to be moved out to the railhead at Silver Creek. It was a nice little set-up, and knowing how close this camp was to the trail, he reckoned he was on pretty sure ground in believing that there would be another attempt to get away with more of these cattle.

They rode slowly back to the camp, the fire clearly visible in the darkness. That fire would give away their position, Rad thought, eyeing it closely, and turning the thought over in his mind. He made to mention it to Meekin, then stopped. It might be that the fire could be used to trap any rustlers. With their man dead, shot to prevent him from talking, they would probably try to take the men at the camp by surprise, knowing that the minute they started bunching part of the herd, they would have half a dozen men or so on their necks. They would have to take care of the crew here first.

Stepping down from the saddle, he moved in towards the fire, held out his hands to the warmth. The night air had been bitterly cold, the stars frostily clear in the heaven's firmament.

'How are things out there? Any sign of trouble?' asked Carrico, speaking up from the tongue of one of the wagons.

'Nothing so far,' muttered Meekin. He rubbed his beard. 'We'll take it in turn to go on watch. You take the first spell, Carrico, then I'll go out for a couple of hours.' He glanced at Rad. 'You feel up to takin' a spell, Lobart?'

'Sure, sure. I don't mind. I guess that so long as I'm on the payroll, I have to do my share.'

'All right. I'll wake you when I come in.' He glanced round at the others. 'The rest had better get some sleep. We may be woken up durin' the night by trouble.'

He paused to let the meaning of his words sink in, then moved off and hauled his blanket from the back of one of the trucks, stretched it out near the fire. Carrico came forward with an armful of brush and dropped it on to the flames, kicking the sticks and twigs down with his boot so that they caught immediately, sending red sparks flying high into the still air where they hung like a swarm of fire-flies before winking out.

Rad pulled his own blanket some distance from the fire, well beyond the red glow, in the shade of one of the wagons. Carefully he checked his guns, then placed them under the blanket where he could reach them at a moment's notice. It was possible that there would be no attack that night, but the mere fact that Clem Blanders was undoubtedly somewhere in the vicinity made it seem probable.

He heard a quick murmur of conversation from close to the fire, then the sound of Carrico moving out towards his mount, climbing into the saddle with a creak of leather. A pause, then the other rode slowly out of the camp, the sound of hoofbeats fading slowly into the deep stillness of the night.

The minutes ticked slowly by into an eternity. The fire crackled faintly as more of the dry brush was consumed by the hungry flames. One of the horses shifted a little, making slight sounds in the stillness. Over Rad's head the bright stars wheeled in their eternal circles, constellations rising from the eastern horizon and drifting smoothly across the sky to the west. He recalled how often he had lain in his blankets and watched this grand march of the stars, wondered inwardly about them, what they were, how distant and how large, and even the thinking about it had brought a strange kind of peace to his mind, had made him realize just how trivial and inconsequential all of the problems of men were when viewed against such a majestic background. Time could mean nothing in that great scheme of things, he reflected. Petty quarrels, even the death of a man, were as nothing.

Still thinking these deep thoughts, he fell asleep, woke to a touch on his shoulder, came upright at once, swiftly and quietly, finding Meekin bending over him.

'Past two o'clock,' murmured the other. 'Nothin' stirring out there.'

Rad nodded, threw back the blankets, thrust the guns into their holsters and moved out towards his horse, saddled up, and rode out to the herd. As Meekin had said, it was very quiet here, with nothing stirring, and so it was through the rest of the night.

6

Rustler's Moon

Morning, and the work of the line crew went on as usual. There was the wire fence to be checked and mended where it had been trampled by the rustled herd of a few nights before. Rad took his part in stringing the wire between the heavy wooden posts hammered firmly into the ground. It was hard work, monotonous and mean in the rolling heat of midday and, to add to their difficulties, a wind storm blew up during the late morning, bringing sand and dust off the wastelands to the north, rolling in a cloud of stinging grains of sand that almost blotted out the sun entirely, until it glowed redly and wickedly through the haze that swirled about them. The sand and dust worked its way into every crevice, into their clothing and between their shirts and their flesh, itching and burning and irritating.

They worked with their neckpieces reversed and around their mouths and nostrils in an attempt to keep it out, but somehow the sand managed to work its way into the folds of their skin, across their foreheads and the bridges of their noses, into their eyes and mouths, until they gagged and choked on it.

By late afternoon they had completed one mile-long stretch of wire. There was still more to do but with the storm reluctant to blow itself out, they were forced to give up and make their way back to the camp, where Carrico had a meal waiting for them. He had built a fresh fire in the shelter of one of the wagons, was striving to cook the meat and brew the coffee without too much sand getting into it.

One glance was enough to tell Rad that the cook was fighting a losing battle, but they were all so hungry and thirsty that they would have taken anything and considered it to be the food of the gods. Crouched with his back to the hot, keening wind, Rad drank down the coffee and chewed on the beef after shredding it with his knife blade.

There was one question still uppermost in their minds, but it was Carrico who put it into words. Without looking up, he said: 'They didn't come last night, you figure they may wait until tonight?'

'They could come any time,' Rad said, before Meekin could speak. 'If this storm blows itself out before sunset, then there's a good chance they will. They may figure we've had too much trouble durin' the day to bother keeping a close watch tonight.'

'And if the storm doesn't blow itself out?' Meekin asked.

Rad swallowed a strip of beef, shrugged his shoulders. 'Then I doubt if they'll try anythin'. It'd be foolish of them to try to take a bunch from the herd while those cattle are so edgy.

They could easily start a stampede, and that would mean trouble for them.'

Carrico lifted his head, peered off to the west and north. The sun was going down with a sullen red glow about it, but it seemed that the sky was beginning to clear far down close to the horizon, as if there was a narrow band of colour there which was not touched by the blurring fingers of the storm.

A few moments later Rad was convinced that the tail end of the storm was now lifting clear of the distant horizon, that the rushing wind was carrying the last of the dust and sand across the pasture, and within an hour at the most the storm would be past.

As he watched, the sun came out, shining more brightly than it had since high noon, although it was nearly on the horizon now. The wind still blew as strongly as before, but the air was clearing and the faint rustle of the sand as it drove against the flapping canvas of the wagons was fading appreciably.

When it was past and they could

breathe normally again, it was almost dark. The stars were just beginning to show and Carrico had built up the fire so that the haze of warmth was spreading out in all directions. Rad rubbed at his face where the sand seemed to have scoured the flesh until it felt hot and raw. There was a faint smear of blood on the back of his hand and he got slowly to his feet and walked over to the tub, bent and sluiced the cold water over his face and neck. It stung his skin, cracked the mask of dust which had formed there, but it made him feel fresher than before. The dark curtain of the storm rolled off to the east, revealing the blanket of stars that were wonderfully bright and close.

In the west the moon was visible, a faint yellow scratch that gave very little light. The first sign of the moon he had seen for several days, he recalled. As they had feared, the cattle were restless and edgy. The storm had upset their usually placid nature and they began milling around uneasily as Rad and

Carrico rode out to bed them down for the night.

'Funny critters,' Carrico said, turning his head slightly. 'You can move them through a thunderstorm with lightning spooking across the heavens and purple flashes darting from their horns, and they won't make a wrong move. And at other times, even a yell can start them runnin'.'

Rad nodded, let his gaze wander over the herd as they moved around, first in a wide circle that was constantly narrowing under the crush of the others. As he lifted his head to peer off into the distance beyond the herd, he caught the faint movement at the very edge of his vision. Swinging his glance around to look directly at it, he saw nothing, wondered if it had been a trick of the light, or whether his imagination was playing tricks with him. Then he saw it again, and knew he had not been mistaken. Narrowing his eyes, he tried to make out what it was.

'Somethin' wrong?' asked Carrico,

edging his mount over beside him.

'There's something movin' yonder, on that ledge about three miles away,' Rad said harshly. 'A man on horseback, I think, though I can't be sure. But if it is, then it could mean trouble. It could be a scout watchin' the herd, making a quick look over the camp while there's still light to see by.'

'Reckon we ought to warn the others?'

'I don't think we'll have trouble for another hour or so. They won't try anythin' until they're sure they can take us by surprise. Besides, they'll wait until it's real dark before they move in.'

'Could be that you're wrong, of course. That might not have been one of them.'

'Maybe.' Rad's voice was non-committal. 'But I don't think so.'

★ ★ ★

It was dark enough in the hills to hide any little movement, and the moon threw scarcely any light over the country. Rad stood well outside the glow of the fire, letting his gaze roam in every direction, not sure from which direction the first hint of trouble would come. From somewhere close at hand there came a long, low, mournful cry, wailing up and down a weird scale, sending a little shiver along his spine. A coyote greeting the moon, or the call of one of those rustlers in the hills. From somewhere a little closer at hand the call was repeated and this time he felt sure that it had not been a coyote. Meekin turned from where he sat on the tongue of the nearby wagon, his Winchester held tightly between his hands.

'Sounds like them,' he said, nodding. 'Could be you were right.'

'You got the others posted?'

Meekin nodded again. 'They know what to do,' he said quietly, grimly. 'But if there are too many — '

'If they come in force, then there may be nothing we can do,' Rad told him

253

softly. 'My guess is that they'll figure we can be taken by surprise. Could be they decided not to attack last night just to make us feel secure.'

'If they do come in, my guess is they'll come from the north. That way they could get real close, moving down from the foothills and — '

He broke off sharply as Rad reached out, gripped him tightly by the arm, fingers biting into the other man's flesh even through his jacket and shirt. The moon hung tilted in the west now, so thin that there was scarcely any glow from it at all, and somewhere off to the north there came the distinct run of a horse, headed in their direction. He listened as the horse came on, wondered for a moment. This rider was making no secret about his approach. He came unhesitatingly forward until a while later he showed up at the edge of the fireglow.

Meekin stepped forward out of the shadows near the Conestoga, the rifle lined up on the other. The man reined his horse. For a long moment there was silence. From his position to Meekin's rear, Rad eyed the other closely. He did not recognize the man as anyone he had seen in Lawless, but that was no assurance that this was not one of Pannard's men.

'Spotted your fire from the hills and rode over,' said the other easily. 'I could do with a spot of food if you've any to spare. Got money here to pay for it if you like.'

Very slowly, Meekin lowered the rifle. He was still suspicious, but some of the unsureness was beginning to leave him. Rad remained where he was, still suspecting a trick. He watched closely as the man slid down from the saddle and walked over to the fire, holding out his hands to the blaze. He had a sly, crafty face, with close-set eyes and the stubble of several days on his face. Crouching down, he glanced about him, his keen eyes taking in everything. Rad noticed the guns slung low on the other's hips, the furtive manner in which he turned his head, as if making sure that he saw everything there was to be seen.

Meekin moved over to the fire, jerked a thumb towards the pan with a couple of slices of beef still in it. 'Help yourself, mister,' he said quietly. 'We have plenty. No need to pay for this.'

'Thanks.'

The other fished the slices of beef from the pan, slid them on to a plate and teased the meat with his bowie knife. He chewed thoughtfully on it for several moments without speaking, then said, conversationally: 'That your herd I noticed out yonder on the hill?'

'No. Belongs to the Bar X ranch. This is their line camp.'

The other nodded, continued eating for a little while longer. Presently he set down the empty plate, ran the back of his hands over his lips. Then he poured coffee into a cup and set it to his lips, not lowering it until he had drained it dry. Reaching forward, he poured a second cup, sat back on his heels. 'It looks to be a mighty fine herd. Must be all of three thousand head there. Surely you got more men watchin' it than yourself.'

'There are more out yonder, circling it right now,' answered Meekin easily. He walked across to the wagon and leaned his shoulders against one of the uprights. 'You been ridin' long?' he inquired, rolling a smoke.

'Ten days. Headin' west into California. Heard there was land and gold there for the asking.'

'Wouldn't know about that,' Meekin said, thrusting the cigarette between his lips. He lit it and drew deeply on it. 'But I do know that there's a lot of bad territory to cross before you get to California. Steer clear of Lawless if you're headed that way.'

'Lawless?' The other glanced up, a faintly cynical smile on his lips. 'That a town?'

'That's right. Run by a *hombre* called Pannard, Ed Pannard. He's a killer and he has a bunch of hired killers riding for him.'

'Ain't you scared he might decide to try for this herd if he's that big?'

'He's tried. Got away with a handful a few nights ago. Doubt if he'll try it again.'

The man at the fire shrugged, then looked down at the empty cup in his right hand. He sat like that for a long moment, his head bowed forward a little, cocked slightly on one side, almost as though he were listening for something. Then he placed the empty cup down on the ground beside him and pushed himself to his feet. 'Guess I'll hobble my horse,' he said softly and moved away from the fire.

Rad, standing well in the shadows of the wagon, out of sight of the other, watched closely as the man stepped close to his mount, reaching up as if to slip the reins over the animal's head. There was something about the other's attitude that troubled him and his right hand hovered close above the butt of the Colt in its holster. He had the feel of danger in his mind. It was a purely instinctive feeling, one that he could not explain.

The man remained quite still beside his mount, his head turned so that he was looking out into the black circle of the night that lay beyond the light of the fire. Then suddenly and without warning, gunshots flared in the night. Rad jerked the gun from its holster, lined it up on the man standing just inside the fireglow.

Even as the hard echoes of the shots were dying away, the man had pulled the Winchester from its scabbard and was swinging to line it up on Meekin. Out of the corner of his eye, Rad saw Meekin suddenly realize his danger, how he had been tricked. He moved back, hands diving for the guns at his waist, but he would have been miles too slow.

The Winchester was almost lined up on him when a single shot rang out. The man staggered as though he had been pushed in the chest by an invisible fist. For a moment he strove to keep the life in his eyes, bracing his legs wide, back resting on the flanks of the fidgeting horse, his arms struggling to lift the rifle which now seemed to weigh a ton, to be far too heavy for him to hold. He turned slowly in a half circle. Then the rifle slipped from his fingers, clattered to the ground in front of him and, as his horse shied away at the sudden racket, he slipped to his knees, head tilted back a little, a look of utter surprise written over his features. His lips were drawn back over his uneven teeth and he tried to bring one hand up to touch the red stain that spread into the cloth of his shirt. Almost the fingers reached it. Then he slumped forward on to his face in the dirt, arms outspread, fingers raking into the dust in that last fight against death.

Rad moved quickly into the middle of the camp. Meekin stared down in surprise at the dead man, then swung on Rad.

'It's a good thing you stayed where you were,' he said tautly, his voice lifted a little in pitch and volume. 'He came here to kill me the minute the attack started.'

'No time to worry about that,' Rad said thinly. Jerking a hand towards the herd, he called: 'There's trouble out there and we'd better get out and see what it is.'

He leapt into the saddle, pulled his horse's head around and rode out of the camp with Meekin close on his heels. Darkness closed swiftly in on them from all sides. The camp fire was behind them, forgotten now. Shots sounded in a ragged, uneven rhythm on all sides. Guns flared in the darkness with stilettos of yellow flame tulipping from their barrels.

Rad caught a glimpse of the bunch of dark shapes that came bearing down on him out of the night. He raised his gun, lined it up and squeezed the trigger, saw one man throw up his arms and drop from the saddle. The crash of the shot sounded in sharp contrast to the angry bellow of the steers. At any moment now, he knew, they could take it into their heads to stampede and then they would have real trouble on their hands. Maybe this was what the rustlers were waiting for. Once the herd began to run, once there were countless tons of beef and muscle headed across the pasture, it would be a simple matter for them to cut a bunch of steers from the stampeding herd and drive them off while he and the rest of the men who guarded the herd were busily engaged in trying to round up the main group.

A bullet hummed past his head as he pulled himself low in the saddle, drilling his heels into the horse's flanks, urging it forward. There were more rustlers working their way in from the north. He caught a brief glimpse of them heading diagonally towards the rear of the herd. Swerving his horse so violently that it almost went down on to its knees, he headed it towards them, firing as he rode. Two men toppled sideways from their saddles. One dropped under the flailing hooves of his own mount. The other, his foot locked in a stirrup, was dragged along the ground as his horse panicked and swung away to one side, heading away from the herd.

There was more firing over on the far side of the herd where Carrico and two others were stationed. The cattle bellowed their protest as the shots sounded around them. Wheeling his mount, Rad closed with two of the rustlers as they swung their horses diagonally across the face of the herd, guns blazing in the eyes of the steers, trying to force a bunch away from the rippling mass of shadows and out across the plains. His horse crowded with that of one of the men and he saw the man turn in his saddle with a look of anger and alarm on his dull features. It was one of the men who had held up the stage and taken him off to that cabin in the hills. A man with a brushy chin and narrowed eyes. Then the other lifted his gun, aimed it straight at Rad and pulled the trigger. For a split second everything seemed to stand still as Rad tensed himself for the inevitable bullet. But it never came. There was a sharp click as the hammer of the Colt fell on a spent cartridge. The man uttered a harsh oath, drew back his arm and hurled the gun straight at Rad's head as the horse raced on alongside him. Ducking, Rad felt the metal graze the side of his shoulder. A stab of pure agony lanced through his body as the gun struck. Then he aimed and fired in one swift, instinctive movement, saw the man reel in the saddle, throwing up both hands to his face as the slug took him cleanly between the eyes. Then he was gone and the riderless horse raced on into the darkness.

The second man came on, riding low in the saddle. His gun flared once, briefly, in the darkness. Rad felt the scorching touch of the slug on his cheek, then the man hauled on his mount, pulling away, racing it across the front of the snorting, bellowing herd. A steer bawled, then another. The flashes of the guns in their faces was proving too much for them. There was sudden movement, a ripple that spread along the shadowed mass, and abruptly the herd moved into action, snorting and lunging, needle-tipped horns raking everything in their path.

Stampede! The rumble of hoofs as thousands of tons of bone and muscle went on the move blotted out everything else. Even the crashing racket of the guns was drowned in it. Almost with one accord, the entire herd was on the rush towards the distant horizon, spilling in a massive avalanche of flesh and brute strength across the grass.

Out of the corner of his eye Rad saw the rustler who had veered away from him after firing that single shot move into the path of the herd. In spite of himself, he tried to yell a harsh warning to the other, thought he saw the man turn his head at the sudden shout, his face a pale grey blur in the dimness.

Then there was no time even to think. The man realized his danger, tried to spur his mount forward, quartering it across the face of the herd in an attempt to reach the far side before it came crushing and thundering down on him.

He almost made it. He had passed the tip of the crescent formed by the leaders as they plunged headlong across the plain. Rad saw the rider in a series of brief glimpses as his horse struggled valiantly to outdistance the steers on the far side of the mass. Then, in spite of every effort, the outer rim of the herd swung in, sweeping relentlessly forward, blocking his flight. Rad saw him throw up his arms. Then he had vanished under the thundering mass of beef that engulfed him. He was gone in an instant, and the herd rolled over the spot where he had gone down.

A swift glimpse about him and Rad saw that there were no more rustlers on this side of the running animals. Any on the far side would have to be left to

Carrico and the others. All he could do now was to try to swing the herd around, to move them in on themselves and start them milling aimlessly again. That was now the only way to stop this headlong flight of the fear-crazed animals. If he couldn't do it, they would be halfway to hell and Georgia by morning, and it would take several days to round them all up.

The horse matched its speed with that of the lunging beasts, checking a little as Rad leaned from the saddle, ignoring the pointed horns that raked for his legs. His gun splashed flame as he fired into the heads of the nearer steers, dropping several as he tried to build up a dam of bodies to halt the others crowding in on their heels. Meekin was with him, emptying his guns and then slashing fiercely with his riata at the steers, yelling and shouting as he strove to swing them away from their main line of flight and across the face of the others. It was a slow and difficult job, dangerous in that at any moment a further ripple might start further back in the thundering mass and a sudden swerve on the part of the leaders would bring the entire herd down on them without any chance to swing out of the way.

But slowly, gradually, they were succeeding in turning them. The movement was almost imperceptible at first. Then it built up as Rad and Meekin forced them around into a wide circle, started them milling aimlessly. Anything to stop that headlong flight to the distant hills. Time held no meaning as every minute was stretched out into a terrible eternity. There was danger, but no one thought of that.

Slowly the other tip of the herd was swung in, the steers became entangled, mixed, forced to slow their headlong rush. Slower and slower they moved, worn out by their run and, with the leaders hopelessly enmeshed, the stragglers stumbled to a halt and stood trembling while the fear left them and there was only the dull weariness in them. Rad leaned forward in his saddle, his breath coming in harsh, whistling gasps through his lips, rasping in his throat.

Meekin rode up, wiping the sweat from his face where it streamed down his cheeks and forehead, even in the cold chill of the night air. The moon had gone down, and there were only the sharp-bright stars to give any light.

'I reckon they should be all right now,' Meekin said hoarsely.

He stared down at a trampled mass of flesh and bone, a weak steer that had gone down in the crush, or maybe one that had been shot in order to halt the others. It was inevitable that some should have had to be killed in order to save the rest.

'What about those critters who started all of this?' Rad glanced about him, peered into the night as he tried to push his sight through the darkness. A rider drifted forward from the other side of the herd, came slowly up to them. It was Carrico. There was a deep scratch on his face and one of his legs had been gouged by a needlesharp horn, but he gave them a quick grin, reined his stud and jerked a thumb into the distance.

'I guess that stampede brought us more than ten miles from the camp,' he said. 'Reckon we'd better bed down here for the night and check on the herd in the mornin' as soon as it gets light.'

'How about the rest of the men?' asked Meekin tersely. 'Any casualties?'

'I don't reckon so.'

Carrico turned as another man rode up. One of the men who had been riding herd when Rad had joined the camp, he clutched now at a broken shoulder. Carrico edged his mount forward, and helped the other down. 'I'll take a look at that shoulder,' he said quietly. 'First we'd better get a fire goin'.'

Fifteen minutes later a fire was blazing in a small hollow, sheltered by the hills. During all of that time they had seen nothing of the rustlers, and when the count had been taken, it was soon clear that the gunhawks had lost seven men and possibly more had been caught by surprise when the herd had suddenly stampeded and were now no more than tangled heaps of broken, torn flesh on the plain.

Rad sat close to the fire, eyes lidding and closing with weariness as the heat seeped into his tired limbs, relaxing them, loosening taut muscles which seemed to have been knotted for far too long.

Carrico had a pot of water boiling over the flames and began to tend to the injured man, probing for the bullet that was still embedded somewhere in the fleshy part of his shoulder. The wound looked more dangerous than it really was, although the man had lost a lot of blood, and it was a long and painful operation, digging for the piece of metal that had been the cause of the trouble.

Finally the slug was out and Carrico

turned it over curiously in his hands for a moment before tossing it to the man as he bent and began to bind up the shoulder. Not a professional job, thought Rad, such as one of the doctors in Lawless or Silver Creek would have done, but neat and sufficient in spite of that. When a man spent long years on the trail, he inevitably learned how to doctor wounds like these, how to set broken bones, treat snake bites.

* * *

Daybreak found them grouped about the remains of the fire. There was coffee ready, a quick breakfast, and then into the saddle to check the herd. A couple of dozen steers had been killed during the stampede, but the rest were feeding peaceably in the long grass, none the worse for their ordeal. Meekin inspected the herd, then crossed back to the fire and squatted beside Rad.

'We'll move 'em back to their original ground today,' he said. 'Not much damage done and I figure those critters won't be so quick at comin' back after the beatin' they took last night.'

Rad nodded. 'Reckon I'll ride back to the ranch and let Miss Ella know what happened,' he said finally. 'That was mainly why she sent me here. Could be they might try somewhere else now that they've failed here. Pannard won't give up his attempt to gain control of the Bar X ranch just because of this one setback. Besides, I'd like to know where that *hombre*, Blanders, is right now. I'd thought he might have been leading that attack last night, but nobody seems to have seen him.'

'He wasn't with those men,' Meekin stated positively. 'He probably figures that he'd set up this attack when he killed Anderson, the only man who could have talked; maybe he expected no trouble.'

Rad nodded, musing inwardly. He felt a little nagging sense of worry deep inside him. Once Pannard learned that not only had this rustling attack failed, but that he had lost so many of his men, he might decide to force a showdown and ride directly out to the Bar X ranch, forcing the issue. The more he thought about it, the more likely that course of action on the other's part seemed to Rad. He felt suddenly restless, anxious to be on his way.

* * *

Rad made good progress along the trail back to the Bar X ranch, passing the spot where Anderson lay buried in the soft earth; a man who had been killed because he had thrown in his lot with the wrong sort of men and had learned too late that they were not to be trusted, that they only used a man for their own ends and when his usefulness ended, his life came to an end also.

The sun lay half-hidden behind a hazy sky as he rode south, with the heat lying pressed close to the ground like a stifling blanket, bringing the sweat out on his face and the small of his back, his shirt clinging to his flesh, chafing it with every little movement he made. He rode with a rider's looseness about him, eyes quartering the far horizons, watchful and alert, not sure of what he was searching for, but with the feeling of impending disaster in his mind, overriding everything else, crowding out the rest of his thoughts.

Behind him lay league after league of rolling grass, interspersed with patches of grey, flinty soil where very little grew. He crossed a couple of narrow streams that flowed swiftly down from the hills to his left, hills which lay vague behind the shimmering heat haze. Sundown, he figured, should see him back at the ranch.

High noon and he rested on the bank of a narrow river, born in the distant hills and now beginning to swell out and cut its way between high banks, moving swiftly near the banks, but more slowly in the middle, where it was deeper, and the undertow pulled the water around the upthrusting rocks that broke surface in places. He let his horse drink a little. Not as much as it wanted, but he still had a distance to cover, and it was far better to ride dry than to sweat out gallons of water on the trail.

Rolling a cigarette, he thrust it between his lips, took his time to light it. When the smoke was finished, he saddled up once more, rode on through the blistering heat of the afternoon. The arid dust boiled about him, kicked up by his horse's hoofs, hanging motionless in the air at his back, marking out his trail for anyone who might be watching.

But for a long while he saw no one on the trail. Then, over on his right, far distant, he saw a similar pattern of dust where another rider was moving south, ahead of him, riding down off the low ridges that lifted in an irregular outline against the skyline.

Rad watched the dust for several minutes before he felt confident that it was only a solitary rider there, and not a bunch of men. He felt a little easier in his mind, but urged his mount on at a quickened pace.

Shortly before six o'clock the hazy skies cleared and the middle-down sun blazed more strongly than at any other time during the day, shining almost directly into Rad's eyes. He noticed that the rider, who had been to the west of him, had begun to sweep in so that he was now almost on the trail in front of Rad but some five or six miles distant. Checking his mount on a rise of ground that looked out over the broad lands around the Bar X ranch, Rad eased himself forward in the saddle. The rider was headed towards the trees that overlooked the cluster of buildings.

Even as Rad watched, eyes narrowed to shut out most of the sunglare, he saw the man vanish into the trees. Waiting, he watched for the other to emerge and continue on the trail, but although he sat there patiently for several minutes, the other did not ride on out of the trees, and Rad urged his horse forward with puckered brows as he tried to figure out the other's actions.

He ran a dry tongue over dry lips. His canteen hung full by his side, but he did not pause to unscrew the top and lift it to his lips. True, there could have been some explanation for what the other had done, but at the moment he could not see it. Certainly there had been nothing familiar about that rider. Distance and darkness beginning to creep in from the eastern horizon put an end to his contemplation of that question.

The ranch was still and quiet as he rode down the side of the hill overlooking the buildings, his tired mount picking its way carefully along the narrow trail past the small herd which grazed on the higher slopes of the hill. As he approached, he eyed the empty corral from beneath lowered lids, let his gaze wander over the dusty courtyard. A thin spiral of grey smoke lifted from the chimney. Nothing seemed amiss, yet the feeling of uneasiness, of danger, still persisted in his mind, bringing caution uppermost in his thoughts. He eased the guns in their holsters. At the bottom of the narrow trail he eased up his mount, paused for a moment, searching about him with eyes and ears. Then he saw the door open and Ella Redden stepped out on to the porch. She swung to face him as he rode across the open courtyard, then stepped down from the porch.

'Was there any trouble at the camp?' she asked, as he turned his horse loose into the corral.

'Some,' he said quietly. 'They came last night, tried to take some of the herd. Unfortunately for them, we were ready. I'd stationed the men on either side of the herd. We cut down seven of them, and others must've been killed by the herd. It stampeded once the shootin' started.'

'Were any of our men killed?' There was a note of concern in her voice.

He shook his head, moved with her

on to the porch. 'One man got a bullet in his shoulder, but Carrico managed to get it out for him. He'll be as good as new in a couple of days.'

He seated himself on the step beside her, relishing the coolness of the air that flowed against him.

'One man was killed, although he wasn't one of those on the payroll. Seems he rode into the camp a few days ago and asked for a job. Meekin gave him one, intending that he should come here and fix things up with you once he'd proved himself. He was on his way back to do that when he was shot down from cover. I saw it happen and he was still alive when I found him.'

'Shot?' The girl's eyes widened. 'But why should anyone want to — '

'I've been thinkin' about that,' Rad said softly. 'This man, Anderson, managed to tell me that it was Clem Blanders who'd been trailin' him all day, and it must've been him who fired the shot. I guess that Anderson had been put into your camp to get information from Meekin and the others, information which he fed back to Pannard so that the other would know when and where to attack. That was how they managed to rustle off part of the herd a few nights ago without the men there being any the wiser. Anderson was on guard and he failed to raise the alarm.'

'But why did they kill him if he was helping them?' asked the girl, perplexed.

'Because they were afraid once he arrived here to see you, he might talk. So far, we have no concrete evidence that Pannard is at the back of this rustling. Nothin' that would stand up in court, anyway.'

'I see. But Anderson could have given us that information.'

'Yes. Now he's dead, and dead men tell no tales.'

'And those men who attacked the herd. Did you recognize any of them?'

'One man,' Rad admitted. 'He was one of the men who held up the stage and took me into the hills.' He rubbed his chin. 'He was trampled to death by the herd when they stampeded.'

'So we still have nothing to go on.'

'I'm not so sure.' Rad glanced towards the trees that grew thickly on top of the hill in the distance. 'Did anyone come ridin' into the ranch about two hours ago. One of the outriders, perhaps?'

The girl glanced at him for a moment, concentrating. Then she shook her head decisively. 'I'm sure no one did. I would have heard them if they had ridden in. But there's been no one for the whole of the afternoon. Bill and Chuck are with the herd on the hill yonder, been there all day. If either of them had ridden back they would have come in to tell me.'

'It certainly wasn't either Bill or Chuck,' Rad said, puzzled. The imp of suspicion flared again inside his mind. 'I spotted this rider shortly after three o'clock, heading this way from the west. He was ridin' fast and I'm not sure whether he spotted me on his trail or not. I watched him all the way into the trees yonder, but he never rode out to come down here. That was mystifying to say the least.'

'Then whoever it was, he could still be hiding out in the trees yonder.' As she spoke, the girl got to her feet and moved over to the window, peered out into the dusk. Rad moved swiftly towards her, pulled her back a little from the window.

'There's just a chance he might be squattin' up there with a Winchester, getting ready to shoot anybody who frames himself in this window,' he said tightly. 'I reckon I'll slip out and take a quick look around.'

'Be careful.'

He looked at her for a moment with a penetrating attention. Then he nodded his head slowly. 'I don't intend to take any chances.'

Slipping out of the door, he moved quickly across the courtyard, took the narrow trail that led up towards the trees, keeping his head down. It was still not dark enough for him to hope to reach the trees unseen by anyone who might be crouched down in the brush there, but he preferred to draw a bullet now while he was still some distance away, than for any hidden gunman to wait until he was close enough for the other to get in a killing shot.

But he reached the outer fringe of trees without incident. Silence crowded around him as he stepped into the green gloom which lay under the trees. There was only the occasional lowing of the herd in the distance as they settled down wearily for the night, and he listened to these sounds with only a part of his mind, focusing almost the whole of his attention on any faint sounds in the undergrowth.

The stillness and dimness lay unbroken in every direction as he edged his way forward, eyes alert, every nerve stretched to its limit. He had one of his guns in his fist now, treading carefully, taking care not to step on a dry twig, for in that stillness it would snap with a sound like a pistol shot that would carry for a long distance.

After a quarter of an hour's slow search, he began to feel that perhaps he had been mistaken when he had imagined the rider he had spotted that afternoon had ridden into these trees and not ridden out again. He had been quite a distance away when it had happened, and the sun had been shining directly into his eyes, half blinding him. And yet he had felt so sure at the time.

Carefully he slipped through the trees, came upon a small clearing, then froze instantly at a sudden sound, a brief movement at the far side of the open stretch of ground. A fire had been lit in the centre of the clearing, and there was still the faint smell of wood smoke in the air, touching the back of his nostrils as he stood there, absolutely motionless.

A moment later, in the gloom, he made out the shape of the horse, standing patiently near the trees, cropping the lush grass which grew right up to their very roots. There was no sign of its rider, but he did not doubt that the horse belonged to the man he had seen that afternoon. Very cautiously he moved around the clearing, watchful for the first sign of danger.

He reached the horse and it shied away from him as he came up to it, then steadied as he spoke softly to it, patting its neck. He was a good judge of horseflesh and he knew this was no mean horse. Inwardly, he had the feeling he had seen it somewhere before and the knowledge ticked at him, a tiny thought that refused to go out of his head. Then it came to him in a flash. This was the horse he had ridden when he had been taken from that cabin in the hills, when he had succeeded in getting away from that bunch of killers and making his way to the Bar X ranch; the horse which had been taken from that empty warehouse in Lawless while he had been talking with Ellis, the newspaper editor. He felt no doubt about it. There could be no doubting a thoroughbred like this.

Then it meant that the man who had ridden it had been one of Pannard's men and that he had ridden here for a purpose. It became all the more necessary that he should find the man before he had a chance to do any damage. But it seemed clear that he was no longer here in the trees.

A further quick search of the wood revealed nothing and he came out on to the trail again, walking slowly back to the ranch. A yellow gleam of light showed in one of the windows and, in the corral, his horse was still there where he had left it. Evidently the man had not got into the ranch, but there were still several of the other buildings where he might be hiding, biding his time until he considered it safe to come out. Had he come there to kill the girl, or maybe to kidnap her, take her into Lawless where she would then be forced to do as Pannard wished? It was a thought that made his blood run cold in his veins and, acting on impulse, he made his way over to the barn. Everything was still and nothing seemed out of the ordinary.

Carefully he pushed the door open and peered inside. In the gloom he could make out nothing. Then, almost before he was aware of the danger, the man stepped out of the shadows at the rear of the barn, the gun in his hand levelled on Rad's chest. He came forward very slowly, a greyly indistinct figure that stopped when it was less than four feet away.

'I figured you might have seen me this afternoon, Lobart, so I came along here to finish this once and for all.'

'Is this the way you fight, Blanders?' Rad grated tightly, not once removing his glance from the other.

'This is good enough,' grinned Clem thinly. His teeth showed whitely in his face. 'You've caused us far too much trouble and Ed Pannard wants rid of you. He said to take you in alive, but I reckon that could be a mite too dangerous. You got away from us once before and you might do it again. But I don't suppose he'll take it too badly if I take your body in instead. Now move back out of the barn so that your girl friend can see you die.'

7

Death Plays a Hand

For a moment Rad's hands hovered uncertainly above the butts of his guns in their holsters, the thought of action in his eyes. Blanders must have seen it even in the gloom, for he said softly, mockingly: 'Just try it, Lobart. My finger is itchin' to send you into eternity.'

Rad shrugged, backed away, out through the door of the barn and into the courtyard. With Bill and the rest of the men with the herd and only the girl in the ranch house, he knew he could expect little help. His eyes never left the gunhawk's face as he stepped back, lips tight, thinking fast.

'All right, that's far enough,' snapped Blanders, as Rad reached the middle of the courtyard, his back to the house.

Lifting his voice, Blanders called:

'Better step outside, Miss Redden. I've got your friend here and I want you to see what sort of man he is when he's at the wrong end of a gun. Don't try anything funny or I'll shoot him right now.'

There was a pause. Rad saw Blanders glance over his shoulder and then he heard the door of the house open and knew that the girl had stepped out on to the porch.

'That's better,' called Blanders. He eyed Rad viciously, lips tight, thinned back over his teeth. His piggy eyes were narrowed as he moved forward a couple of paces. He said tautly: 'You should have sold this place to Mr Pannard when he made you that offer and then all of this unpleasantness might have been avoided. As it is, you've caused too much trouble. Especially this *hombre* here. You swore you'd kill Pannard, didn't you, Lobart? I wonder why you wanted to do that so badly? You rode into Lawless alone. I've known Pannard for close on fifteen years and I never set eyes on you before that day we took you off the stage, so it must have been something that happened before then. Unless you're one of those bounty hunters, lookin' for the reward.' His eyes narrowed a little, speculatively, then he shook his head slowly. 'No, somehow, I don't think that's it. You're no bounty hunter. You've got more on your mind than that. But it isn't goin' to make any difference now. Like I said, I'm takin' you back to Pannard, only I'm takin' no chances, and you'll go back over the saddle of your horse, with a bullet in you. That way, I'll be sure of everything.'

'Like you were when you shot down Anderson along the trail?' said Rad.

Blanders grinned. 'So you know about that.' He nodded. 'I figured you might have been there at the line camp when the boys attacked last night. Meekin and those others couldn't have faced up to them.'

'It doesn't take much guts to shoot a

man down from cover, to plug him in the back. Any dry-gulcher could do that, and I reckon that describes you pretty well, Blanders.'

'Don't try to rile me, Lobart, because it won't work. You can say what you like right now, because I'll get enough pleasure out of gunning you down to make up for anythin' you have to say. And you won't be able to talk for long. I just want the girl to see you plead for mercy, to see the kind of coward you are at heart. Then I finish you and take you back into town. And as for you, Miss Redden, it won't be long now before Pannard comes ridin' to take over this place, and if you got any sense at all, you won't try to fight.'

'You don't think you'll get away with any of this, do you?' said the girl, her tone sharp. 'Bill!' As she spoke, she turned her head sharply, stared off into the darkness at the edge of the courtyard.

Rad saw Blanders shift his gaze, even though the other must have known it was just a trick, that everyone else was out with the herd that night; he had probably watched them leave before deciding to make his play. But the girl's sudden shout had had enough authority in it to make even him turn his head and glance swiftly, instinctively, in the direction where she had obviously been looking when she had spoken. It was a purely involuntary movement, slight and brief, but it was enough for Rad. Swiftly, without even pausing to think of the odds that were stacked against him, he threw himself sideways, going down on to his side, fingers clawing the gun from his holster as he went down. He seemed to fire the single shot while he was still in mid-air, almost horizontal.

The slug took Blanders in the chest, hurling him back, almost spinning him completely round. He managed to trigger off a solitary shot that ploughed into the dirt at his feet, whining past Rad's head in murderous ricochet. For a moment the killer stood there in stupid fashion, the gun tilting in his fingers. Then it dropped in front of him and he went down, knees buckling gently under him as though all of the strength had evaporated from them, and they were unable to hold him up any longer. Blood came from his mouth with every exhalation as he knelt there, eyes turned to look at the man who had killed him when everything had seemed to be in his favour.

He collapsed suddenly as Rad got to his feet and walked slowly forward, muzzle of his gun lowered to cover the other, but there was no need for a second shot. Blanders' eyes rolled upward until only the whites were showing. He uttered a faint sigh, then lay stretched out in the dust.

Ella Redden stepped down from the porch and walked forward. There was a faint look of horror on her delicate features.

'He was waitin' in the barn,' Rad explained, holstering the still-smoking gun. 'He took me by surprise, had the drop on me the minute I went inside. If you hadn't been quick thinkin', he would have shot me there and then without a chance to defend myself.'

'You think he was telling the truth when he said that Pannard would soon bring his men here to take the place?' she asked, glancing up at him.

'It could be true. Pannard will know now that he can't afford to waste any time. Things are moving against him. He's lost a lot of men in the past few days, and his rustlin' activities haven't been the success he'd obviously hoped. Besides, I got the impression when I was in town that there's a lot of feelin' against him. Once folk there discover that it is possible to stand against him, they may decide to throw off this lawlessness which has oppressed them for so long. And if Pannard was to be killed, it might hurry things on a little.'

He saw the faintly alarmed look which came to her face. 'Are you intending to ride into Lawless again on this errand of death? Wasn't the last time enough warning that you can't hope to fight Pannard alone?'

'I've got to do it. Perhaps one day you'll know why.'

'Can't you tell me?' Her voice was soft, but with an insistent quality to it which he noticed, which stiffened him a little towards her.

'No,' he said quietly, 'I can't. Not now.'

'Go back into Lawless and you'll be killed,' she said harshly. 'Here, at least, you stand a chance. I can bring in all of the men, gather more than forty at the ranch, and if Pannard does send his men to attack, we may be able to hold them off, give better than we get. Once we've destroyed most of his men, then you may have a chance of getting at him on even terms.'

'That isn't possible,' Rad said quietly, evenly. 'Sooner or later, Pannard is going to start askin' himself some questions, and when he does he may find out who I am, and then he'll throw over everything to get me. Believe me, you don't know anythin' about this at all, at the moment.'

She seemed to draw away from him slightly at that, then she said with a trace of stiffness in her voice: 'I know that if I hadn't saved your life a little while ago you'd be lying where that man is now.' She nodded towards Blanders' body in the courtyard. 'If you were to ride into Lawless, you may still end up the same way.'

Rad shrugged. 'That may be true,' he agreed. 'But I have to do this.' He was thinking of Ed Pannard as he spoke, feeling the intense hatred for the man that existed within him, something which had grown over the years and the months until it was a burning flame inside him that would never give him peace.

'Very well, then.' Ella Redden tossed her head imperiously. 'If you think so little of your life that you want to throw it away, ride into Lawless and try to hunt this man down. Don't expect me to stop you or cry after you when you're dead.'

She turned abruptly from him and ran into the house, slamming the door behind her. For a long moment Rad stood there in the quiet stillness of the courtyard, knew that she was crying inside the house. Then he whirled abruptly on his heel, whistled up his horse from the corral and busied himself putting on the saddle, getting his gear ready, bending to tighten the cinch. He did not hear the girl when she came out of the house again, walking silently across to him, much too absorbed in his work. Not until she stood beside him and he smelled the faint perfume of her hair, did he realize she was there. He straightened and looked down into her eyes, thought he saw tears there, but could not be sure in the darkness.

She reached out a tentative hand and laid it on his arm. 'I'm sorry for what I said a few minutes ago,' she murmured softly. 'I wasn't thinking. I suppose I saw a lot of this with my father. He was like you in a great many ways. Nobody scared him. He knew what was right and went ahead and did it, no matter who or what stood in his way. It was this that killed him and I suppose I'm afraid that it will do the same for you.'

'Would it make much difference to you if it did?' he asked hoarsely.

She paused, lips laid close together, eyes wide, looking up into his. Then she murmured quietly: 'I think it would make all the difference in the world, Rad. I know I shouldn't be saying this when you've obviously made up your mind to ride out into town tonight, but I can't help the way I feel. I think I knew it that first night I saw you, when those men were riding after you, hunting you down. That's why I refused to believe them when they said you had been caught trying to rustle their cattle.'

'I'm glad that somebody believed me,' he said harshly.

'Will you ride back if you finish this chore?'

'I'll come back,' he promised. 'With Pannard dead, I doubt if the others will start any trouble. He's the man behind it all. Even Abbott means nothing without Pannard.'

There was an instant while her eyes searched his face as if trying to read what was so well hidden behind his eyes. Then she gave it up, and a little sigh escaped her. 'I love you, Rad,' she said. It was as simple as that. 'I've never loved another man. I know I never will.'

'I'll come back,' he said again. He moved to climb into the saddle. Before he could do so, she had reached up on tiptoe. Her lips brushed his for just a moment, and then she stepped back a couple of paces, watching him intently, as if reluctantly she had let him go for just a little while so that he might have the chance to burn this terrible need for revenge out of his mind and soul.

★ ★ ★

He rode with the night wind, across the flat plains and the rising hills, over the broad mesa and across the sluggishly flowing river, with the water splashing around the horse's legs as it plunged across and climbed up the steep bank on the far side. There was no need to ride off the main trail and head up into the hills on this occasion. He stayed with the stage road where it wound over the desert to the north of the mesa, linking up with the trail that led into the hills five miles further on. In front of him, less than half an hour away, lay Lawless. Now it was completely dark, with the scratch of yellow moon in the west, swinging on its back, giving only a little light. It would set soon and leave the night to the brightly-gleaming stars which were scattered like the silver grains of sand across the sea of the heavens.

He kept his eyes moving instinctively, watching for trouble, but expecting none along this stretch of the trail. Maybe Pannard was in Lawless, in one of the saloons at that very moment, waiting for Blanders to bring him in, hands tied behind his back, as his prisoner. Maybe he had even resigned himself to the fact that Blanders would take no chances and would kill him before bringing in his body for identification, but whatever it was, Pannard would be reasonably sure that he would cause no further trouble.

In a way, he knew he was banking on this being the case. It would mean that Pannard would not be quite as watchful as he might otherwise have been. He would not be expecting Rad to ride openly into town and come looking for him. As he rode, Rad turned all of these thoughts over in his mind, trying to form a plan. He knew that it would not be easy to get Pannard alone. The man was surrounded by paid killers, hired to carry out Pannard's orders and to protect him.

Reaching the hill that overlooked the town, Rad circled Lawless, tracing his way parallel to the main road. From where he finally reined his mount, he was able to look down on to the rooftops of the buildings on either side of the main street and the other that ran at right angles to it, forming the open square in the centre of town. The two roads showed clearly against the darker background of the houses and saloons, bright streaks of dust which glowed palely in the night, picked out in gold here and there where the lights from the windows fell slantwise on them. He noticed several horses parked in front of the saloons, and there was another bunch, with a buckboard, in front of the hotel. One horse stood sleepily in front of the sheriff's office, tied to the hitching rail. Abbott's mount, he thought idly, giving it a quick brush with his glance. Evidently the sheriff was in his office, expecting no trouble. The town seemed remarkably quiet for that time of night. One usually expected a little noise and merriment, with guns flashing as the men worked off their high spirits, riding up and down the main street. But there seemed to be nothing like that. The fact struck him forcibly and he sat forward in the saddle, bending forward a little to take in everything that went on below him.

Presently one of the doors of the saloon swung open and the dark figure of a man staggered out. He walked, swaying drunkenly, along the middle of the street, swerved around one of the tethered horses, almost fell and then continued on into the shadows on the edge of town. Just a drunk, thought Rad inwardly. The thought of Pannard somewhere down there disturbed him anew. He knew that he was wasting precious time up here, watching everything that was going on, but taking no action. Yet he had the unshakeable feeling that if he only stayed here long enough he might be able to see something he could turn to his own advantage.

Patience turned him to a man of stone. He rolled himself a smoke, drew the smoke from the cigarette deep into his lungs. Another bunch of men came out of one of the saloons, made for their mounts, saddled up and rode out of town, taking the road to the north. If he remembered rightly, Pannard's spread was somewhere in that direction. They looked as though they could have been some of his crew. If that was so, why had not Pannard come out with them? The dull abrasion of the riders faded into the distance and everything was silent again. Then, as he flicked the butt of his cigarette away, he saw the man come out of the hotel at the corner of the square and move over towards the rig, climbing up on to the buckboard and taking the reins in his hands.

Rad felt his fingers clench so tightly that the nails dug painfully into the palms of his hands, although he scarcely felt the pain. The man down there was Ed Pannard and he was alone, unsuspecting, thinking nothing of trouble. His men had ridden off to the ranch ahead of him. Rad watched tensely as the other turned the rig in a wide circle around the square and then drove off along the main street in the wake of his crew.

A quick glance told Rad that there was a way down off the hill that would meet the road leading north. Kicking the horse's flanks, feeling the tension begin to climb in his mind, stiffening his limbs a little, he rode on down the slope, the soft earth deadening the sound of his mount's hoofs as he came closer to where the road out of town joined the hill trail.

He was halfway along the trail when he saw Pannard lean forward and slash at the four horses in the traces with the long whip. They lunged forward and the rig increased its speed, wheels churning as it rattled swiftly along the trail into the darkness. Putting his mount down the slope, Rad dug rowels into its flanks. He did not think that Pannard had seen him. The other had acted instinctively. Nevertheless, there was a chance he might manage to get away from him again. If he once caught up with his men somewhere ahead of him, Rad's chances of taking him were slim indeed.

Reaching the trail, he swung his mount on to it, raced after the rig. He could just make out the sound of it somewhere ahead of him, although it was not possible to see it. Spurs rowelled in right to the shanks, he forced the horse along the trail. It drew back its lips and bared its teeth to the night darkness and its tail came up defiantly, streaming out like a pennant behind it. Twice he almost ran the horse off the trail as he strove to see where he was going. He could hear the sound of the rig directly ahead of him, knew he had shortened the intervening distance, and that Pannard had probably heard him by now, knew he was being followed. But perhaps, he reasoned, the other would not know whether it was trouble that came close on his heels, or one of his own men striving to catch up with him.

He pushed his sight into the darkness, then managed to make out the shape of the rig, guessed it was perhaps half a mile ahead of him, lifting a cloud of dust which partially obscured it, but enabled Rad to pick out its position more easily than otherwise.

A quarter of a mile and now he was able to make out Pannard's face as the other turned and peered behind him, trying to make out the identity of the rider following him. He must have realized that it was not one of his own men for he suddenly leaned forward and began slashing at the horses with the whip, urging them to still greater efforts. Slowly Rad closed the distance. He saw Pannard give another quick look over his shoulder. Then the other wheeled sharply on the reins and pulled the gig off the trail, heading out over the rougher country that lay to his right. The move took Rad completely by surprise. Bumping and swaying dangerously, the rig bounced over the uneven ground. Savagely he hauled on the reins, bringing his own mount to a slithering halt. The animal went back on to its hind legs and remained still for a few seconds, then he had swung off the trail and was heading after the rig. It was more difficult to see it here. On the trail there was always something definite to follow but here there was nothing. He could only follow his ears, knowing that he had lost valuable ground by the other's abrupt move. He cursed himself under his breath. Sitting low in the saddle, making it as easy as he could on the horse, knowing that here there would be gopher holes and other invisible obstacles, any of which could snap a foreleg cleanly in two, pitching both horse and rider, he stabbed his eyes into the clinging darkness. In the long grass which grew here there was no chance of seeing any of the gopher holes in time and he knew he had to take his chance and pull the horse ahead at full gallop.

A few moments later he topped a low

rise, found himself looking down into a broad valley which glowed faintly in the shimmering starlight. He spotted the rig almost at once, racing across the valley towards the far side. This could, for all he knew, be a short cut to Pannard's ranch. He did not think the other had pulled off the trail at that particular spot just to gain a few precious yards on him. Pannard was no fool and he would have realized that on rough ground such as this, if a rider was sufficiently determined, a single horse could make far better time than four horses pulling a rig. There was also the very real danger of losing a wheel on rough, uneven ground such as this.

Body well forward, kneeing the horse, Rad pushed it down the slope. It went down with its forelegs stiffened, almost down on its haunches in places, small stones rattling down around it. Reaching the bottom, it plunged forward without altering its stride. Here and there were stunted brush and pine and he was forced to pull his way through them, slowing now and again whenever he ran into thicker timber. Clearly Pannard knew this country like the back of his hand, for he seemed to be having no difficulty in making his way across the valley.

Then, in the stillness of the night, he heard the sharp crack, the sudden splintering of wood as one of the wheels on the gig struck an upthrusting stone and split in two. The gig tilted, lifted precariously into the air on one side as the horses continued to pound forward. He fancied he heard Pannard shout out with a harsh, high-pitched yell. Then the gig went over with a rending crash of splintering wood. The shafts broke free and the horses raced forward.

There was a sudden elation in Rad's mind. Perhaps it was this that proved his undoing. He failed to notice the tree that loomed up without warning in front of him. Instinctively the horse shied away from it, struck its foreleg in a deep depression in the ground and went down. He tried to get his feet free of the stirrups in that split second before tragedy came, almost made it. Then the horse was down, the blow of striking the ground almost knocking him cold. He struggled to free his right leg as the injured animal threatened to roll over on him, somehow managed to jerk it loose and roll away.

His leg felt numb where he had struck it against a boulder and he felt it gingerly. No bones seemed to be broken but there was blood on his fingers as he took them away, blood from a deep cut in his flesh. Gritting his teeth, he fought down the waves of unconsciousness that threatened to sweep over him, to engulf him. He had to keep conscious, had to go on and find Ed Pannard, wherever he might be and exact the justice which he had been owing the other for more years than he could remember.

This was not justice merely for himself. He recalled that well-thumbed book which had been in his saddle-bag all these years, something he had never dared to let out of his sight because it was the one thing which had kept him going, which had been the driving force behind everything he had done. He could recall almost every word that had been written in it, although the ink was faded now after all these years and in places, where water had got at it, the words had been almost wiped clean from the pages.

But it could still tell its own story of betrayal and suffering to anyone who cared to take the trouble to read it, to digest what was written in it. He had it now, tucked away in his pocket. He reached in and curled his fingers about it and suddenly found the strength to force himself up on to his feet, standing swaying for a moment, until he was able to move forward, dragging his injured foot behind, wincing every time he placed his weight on it.

In front of him he could just make out the shape of the splintered rig, but there was no sign of the man who had been driving it. Cautiously, with his gun in his right hand, he approached it, expecting a shot at any moment. But nothing seemed to move and he went forward until he came right up to it, peering into the tangled mass of wood and metal.

He had half-expected to see the unconscious body of Ed Pannard lying inside the smashed rig, but it was empty as he came up to it and, a second later, there was the bark of a pistol and a stiletto of flame from among the rocks a few yards away, and the slug tore into the wood within inches of his body. Savagely, he threw himself down, lying flat in the rough grass, holding his head low, not daring to lift it. Then he heard Pannard's voice from the rocks.

'That's you there, isn't it, Lobart? I thought it might be you. I've had the feelin' that, in spite of all his bragging how fast he was, Blanders wouldn't be able to stop you.'

'So he didn't, and now it's your turn,' said Rad grimly.

'Now don't be a fool,' said the other

quickly. 'I don't know what your part is in this, nor why you're so set on killin' me. I don't know you, I don't recall ever meetin' you. Just what sort of grudge is it that you've got against me? Maybe there's a way we could sort it out between us. This place is big enough for two men, even men like ourselves and we could split up the territory equably. I'm a rich man and you don't seem to have much money. We can make a deal.' He was talking quickly now, the words tumbling over each other as he tried to force his point over to the other. Rad listened carefully all the time the other was talking, assessing just where he was. When Pannard fell silent, he had him placed behind the rocks that lay in a tumbled heap to his right. He fired a couple of shots, heard them strike stone and whine off into the night. Neither found its target in living flesh.

A gun roared from a slightly different direction to where he had placed the other, and he swung his own weapon swiftly to bear on the orange flash. He knew now that as soon as the other had finished talking he had shifted his position.

Carefully, Rad lifted his head, peered about him, taking stock of his situation. Cautiously, he eased himself round the back of the rig, keeping it between himself and the point where he guessed Pannard to be. He felt sure he could crawl forward without being spotted by the other, and come in on him from the flank, where he might be able to take him by surprise. He knew the other was jittery now, that he had been caught at a disadvantage and was striving to think of a way out of his predicament.

'You still want to make that deal, Lobart?' yelled Pannard. His voice seemed oddly muffled as if he was trying to disguise his whereabouts. 'I've got money and you could have one of the ranches if you cared to stay in these parts. Might even let you run one of the saloons.'

'You don't ever forget the sort of man

you are, do you?' called Rad tightly, disgust in his tone. 'I suppose you never could change, even after all these years.'

A pause, then: 'I don't know what you're talkin' about. Just who are you? Lobart isn't your real name, is it? You have some idea I've wronged you and you want revenge. Well, if I have done something against you, and before God I don't know what it is, I'm willin' to make amends.'

'Are you ready to make amends to *her*?' said Rad, speaking through his teeth. 'I didn't know you even existed until a few years ago, when I found her diary. But it was all there. What you did, the way you deserted her, left her to die in that down-and-out shanty in Colorado. You thought you'd get out while you had the chance, you said she was a chain and a burden to you, that you wanted to be free of her. But you'd promised to cherish and love her until death did you part. Yet you couldn't even wait for that. You had to run out and leave her alone.'

He heard the sudden gasp that came from the other, the need for air that had betrayed him, guessed that Pannard now knew exactly who he was and why his offers of money and power meant nothing to him, why there was no power on earth could save him now.

'You're — you're Amy's son. But that was so many years ago. You can't expect me to have remembered that. Your name meant nothing to me, you must've changed it.'

'Just as you conveniently changed yours,' said Rad. 'Maybe you thought even then that retribution might come up on you some day and you wanted to stave off that day for as long as possible. Well, it's here now and I mean to avenge my mother's — your wife's — death. She died because of you, because of what you did, the life you forced her to lead, running from one town to another, never staying in the same place long enough to put down any roots. She was a gentle person, not

319

the sort of woman you wanted for a wife.'

'I swear I never knew. If I'd known I could have — '

'You could have what?' Rad edged forward another couple of feet. He had located the other now, crouched down behind a large boulder, his body a slight shadow in the darkness. 'Would you have gone back?'

'I don't know. A man has to be free and there are times when a woman can be a millstone around his neck. I tried to see that she was well provided for before I left and — '

'You're lyin'!' Rad snapped. 'I found it all written in her diary and I know she had no cause to lie. I've lain awake at nights, when I was only a few years old, and listened to her cryin'. She never knew I heard her, but it would keep me awake night after night. I swore then that some day I'd find you, even if I had to follow you across the whole length of the country, and when I did, I'd make sure you paid for every minute of suffering she endured.'

'Now listen, you've got to hear my side of this. All I wanted to do was to — ' The other broke off. Two shots boomed out from the darkness. Rad pulled himself down sharply as they ricocheted off the rock within an inch of his head. The other had been talking only to make sure of where he was, as a cover for what he intended to do.

Rad kept silent, felt the stillness begin to drag. He knew inwardly that the other would be the first to break. A faint sigh came out of Pannard's lips and a moment later he called: 'I'm comin' out. Don't shoot me in cold blood.'

'Throw out your guns,' Rad said, feeling a little surprise at the other's change of attitude.

A second later he heard the twin thuds as the two Colts were tossed on to the dirt in front of the boulder. Then he saw Pannard get slowly to his feet and edge forward, hands lifted slightly away from his sides. He paused for a moment and then moved out into the open towards the other. Pannard said tightly: 'If you want to shoot me, then go ahead. I guess I deserve everything that's comin' to me for what happened, but it was all such a long time ago and — ' He paused, turned to face Rad as the other stepped down among the boulders that were strewn about. For a moment he seemed to be watching Rad intently, then his hand flashed down, not towards his gunbelt, but to a hidden holster under one arm. Rad was caught off balance, taken by surprise at the other's move, even though he had been half-expecting a trap. He spun, threw himself sideways as the small Derringer roared. He felt the slug pluck at his sleeve as he fell. Then the heavy Colt in his right hand roared twice. He saw Pannard stiffen, then clutch at his chest as he fell forward, the Derringer falling from his fingers. He hit the ground and lay still. Going forward, Rad turned him over with the toe of his boot, relaxed a little as he felt the limpness in the other's body. Bending, he picked up the Derringer, stared down at it for a moment, then tossed it into the brush nearby.

There was a shovel in the smashed wagon and he went back, ignoring the pain in his leg, dug a hole in the soil and placed the body into it. For a moment he stood staring down at the other, then he reached into his pocket, pulled out the diary which he had carried with him all those years, and dropped it on to the other's chest before shovelling the loose soil back in again. He worked slowly, not pausing until the grave was finished and he had topped it off with stones and rocks. He fashioned a crude cross and thrust it into the topsoil, stood for a moment staring down at the grave. He felt a strange peace deep within him, a feeling he had not thought to experience ever again.

Slowly he retraced his steps back towards the trail, knowing that for him this chore was finished, and that it was over for Lawless and the territory around the town. What the men who had followed Pannard would do when they learned of his death he did not know, although he guessed they would ride on over the hills, seeking for some other place where they might find temporary refuge from the law, not knowing that the number of such places was rapidly dwindling as the great exodus of men and women from the east really got under way.

Two hours later he staggered into the main street of Lawless. There were few people abroad at that time of the morning, but his knocking soon aroused the old man Carl, who had sheltered Jake and himself that night that Pannard's men were scouring the town looking for them.

Briefly he explained what had happened, who Pannard had really been. The other listened, then nodded his head. 'I thought it might have been somethin' like that,' he said softly, soberly. 'But I guess it's all over now, both for you and for Lawless.'

Rad thought about that, then nodded. At the moment he felt weary and trail-worn and all he wanted was sleep. But in the morning, he would find a horse and ride out of Lawless, take the trail back west, over the mesa, through the hills, to the Bar X ranch and the girl who was waiting for him.

THE END

We do hope that you have enjoyed reading this large print book.

Did you know that all of our titles are available for purchase?

We publish a wide range of high quality large print books including:
Romances, Mysteries, Classics
General Fiction
Non Fiction and Westerns

Special interest titles available in large print are:
The Little Oxford Dictionary
Music Book, Song Book
Hymn Book, Service Book

Also available from us courtesy of Oxford University Press:
Young Readers' Dictionary
(large print edition)
Young Readers' Thesaurus
(large print edition)

For further information or a free brochure, please contact us at:
Ulverscroft Large Print Books Ltd.,
The Green, Bradgate Road, Anstey,
Leicester, LE7 7FU, England.
Tel: (00 44) **0116 236 4325**
Fax: (00 44) **0116 234 0205**

THE CHISELLER

Tex Larrigan

Soon the paddle steamer would be on its long journey down the Missouri River to St Louis. Now, all Saul Rhymer had to do was to play the last master stroke of the evening. He looked at the mounting pile of gold and dollar bills and again at the cards in his hand. Then, looking around the table, he produced the deed to the goldmine in Montana. 'Let's play poker!' But little did he know how that journey back to St Louis would change his life so drastically.

THE ARIZONA KID

Andrew McBride

When former hired gun Calvin Taylor took the job of sheriff of Oxford County, New Mexico, it was for one reason only — to catch, or kill, the notorious Arizona Kid, and pick up the fifteen hundred dollars reward the governor had secretly offered. Taylor found himself on the trail of the infamous gang known as the Regulators, hunting down a man who'd once been his friend. The pursuit became, in every sense, a journey of death.

BULLETS IN BUZZARDS CREEK

Bret Rey

The discovery of a dead saloon girl is only the beginning of Sheriff Jeff Gilpin's problems. Fortunately, his old friend 'Doc' Holliday arrives in Buzzards Creek just as Gilpin is faced by an outlaw gang. In a dramatic shoot-out the sheriff kills their leader and Holliday's reputation scares the hell out of the others. But it isn't long before the outlaws return, when they know Holliday is not around, and Gilpin is alone against six men . . .

THE YANKEE HANGMAN

Cole Rickard

Dan Tate was given a virtually impossible task: to save the murderer Jack Williams from the condemned cell. Williams, scum that he was, held a secret that was dear to the Confederate cause. But if saving Williams would test all Dan's ingenuity, then his further mission called for immense courage and daring. His life was truly on the line and if he didn't succeed, Horace Honeywell, the Yankee Hangman would have the last word!